The King

The King

Tom Locke

ROUNDFIRE BOOKS

Winchester, UK
Washington, USA

First published by Roundfire Books, 2016
Roundfire Books is an imprint of John Hunt Publishing Ltd., Laurel House, Station Approach, Alresford, Hants, SO24 9JH, UK
office1@jhpbooks.net
www.johnhuntpublishing.com
www.roundfire-books.com

For distributor details and how to order please visit the 'Ordering' section on our website.

ISBN: 978 1 78535 207 2
Library of Congress Control Number: 2015943103

A CIP catalogue record for this book is available from the British Library.

Design: Stuart Davies

Printed in the USA by Edwards Brothers Malloy

Chapter 1

It was just after three o'clock when Vince Kingmyle arrived back at his office. It had, he reflected, been a worthwhile lunch break at the golf club: he'd had a pleasant meal; he'd booked the course for the party of tourists that were due in a couple of weeks; he'd also spent a worthwhile hour talking to that new member, Mike.

Mike seemed like a good fellow, thought Vince. The young man had certainly seemed impressed by the brief biography Vince had given him and had appeared eager to hear the story of Vince's promising football career, so cruelly terminated by injury, and the subsequent success that had followed during his time in the Civil Service and now as a respected local businessman. He also had the impression that Mike would be keen to hear more about the many golf courses Vince had played.

Vince frowned for a moment as he thought of George McDougall. He'd been in the middle of describing the majestic round he'd played at the Celtic Manor course when that old duffer had butted in.

"You're sure one remarkable man, Vince," George had said.

"What do you mean?" Vince had replied, somewhat tetchily.

"Well, golfer, time traveller," George went on, a little self-satisfied smirk on his lips.

Vince had glared at the old fool as he waddled back to his seat with his glass of malt. He found George irritating, but had regained his composure and continued his story.

Jealous as hell, Vince thought, as he paused at the front door of the office. He took out his handkerchief and gave the sign a little polish. It read 'Golf King', the letters of the two words intersected by a large 'V'. Satisfied with its appearance, he went in.

"Good lunch?" asked Krystyna Czerniatynska as he strode to his desk.

Vince, wholly oblivious to the sarcasm in Krystyna's question, said, "Excellent, thank you. I've booked the course for the party from Yorkshire, so put that on the spreadsheet if you don't mind."

Krystyna said, "There are also two other bookings. One group from London and one from Northern Ireland. I have emailed the details to you."

"Tremendous," said Vince, rubbing his hands together. "We're cooking the gas."

Krystyna frowned quizzically, but merely pointed across the room. "And those as well," she said.

Vince looked over at three cardboard boxes. "And they are?" he asked.

"The polo shirts," Krystyna told him. "The 'King of Swing' shirts you wanted."

"Fantastic," Vince said, jumping from his leather swivel chair and pouncing on the boxes in the manner of an overweight cat attempting to catch a woodpigeon. "Yes, yes, yes."

He tore open a box and dug around until he found a large size. "Style with a capital S," he said. He walked across to the door and said, "I will be the model. Excuse me, ladies."

Krystyna glanced at her colleague, Anne, and shook her head. Moments later, Vince was back, wearing the shirt. He walked in front of the two women, performing a small pirouette as he did so. "Stylish, no?" he asked.

"Yeah, it's okay," Anne mumbled. Vince gave her a sharp look.

"Yes, good, very smart," Krystyna said, hurriedly.

"We are literally on fire," Vince said loudly.

Krystyna winced. It was a mental image that was disturbing.

"Perfect," said Vince. "Everyone who books onto a Golf King tour gets one of these to keep. Is that not such a good promotion? It's so brilliant, I don't know why I never thought of it before. It's advertising as well, you see? People will wear these when they get home, they'll wear them at their golf clubs and people will see the 'V' logo and..." He tailed off. Krystyna was staring at him.

"What's wrong?" asked Vince.

Krystyna scampered from behind her desk and grabbed a handful of shirts from the open box as Vince gawped at her in amazement. "Oh, my God," she said.

"What?" Vince demanded.

Krystyna pointed to the lettering that crossed the distinctive 'V' on the shirt's badge. The logo read 'KING OF SWINE'.

Vince's mouth opened, but nothing, other than one or two flecks of spittle, came out. He gaped like a stranded fish for several seconds before diving back into the box and pulling out more shirts. He pulled off the shirt he was wearing and surveyed the lettering. Anne let out a snigger at the sight of her boss's less-than-athletic torso, but fortunately for her, Vince was too preoccupied to hear it.

Naked to the waist, he stormed across the room, flinging the shirt towards the window, where it caught on a plant and remained dangling. "Who," he demanded, "is responsible for this? Who put the order in?"

Anne and Krystyna exchanged glances and Vince, hands on hips and resembling a badly designed teapot, waited for an answer. Krystyna took the plunge. "You did," she said.

Vince, giving a good impression of a man about to be struck down by apoplexy, glared at her and shouted, "Me? Oh, I see. It's my fault. I can't spell the word 'swing', is that what you're telling me?"

"No, I did not say that," said Krystyna in measured tones. "The manufacturers, they must have got it wrong." Vince continued to stare at her before realising his somewhat undignified state of undress and snatching his own shirt from his desk and putting it back on.

Anne, meanwhile, had put her jacket on and Vince looked at her. "Where are you going?" he asked.

"Home. I always go at half three."

"Fine, good, go then."

"Okay, see you tomorrow."

Vince continued to stare at her as she left the office, before turning back to Krystyna. "Are you sure," he asked in a calmer voice, "that it wasn't her? Sometimes I think she's not quite all there."

Krystyna said, "No, sorry, it was definitely you. I remember it, you said that you would take care of it. But the manufacturers must be wrong. They must have made a mistake."

Vince sat down and muttered, "Clowns. That's what you get. Clowns, imbeciles. Can't do anything right unless you do it yourself. When did we order them? I must have the email."

"Four weeks ago, I think," Krystyna told him.

Vince spun his chair around and unlocked a cupboard. He took out a red folder, which was full of email correspondence. Vince, to Krystyna's secret fury, printed out every email that he received. He then placed the print into a clear plastic pocket and put them in a folder. The cupboard was packed with such folders.

He thumbed through the pages and suddenly exclaimed "Ah, got it. Right here. Here we are, email order to Inventive Designs Ltd." He read down the page and suddenly snapped the folder shut before Krystyna, who had appeared beside him, could see the document.

"You found it...so it was the manufacturer?" she asked.

Vince, who had hurriedly rammed the folder back into the cupboard, said, "Yes, yes, of course, idiots, morons." He slammed the cupboard shut and locked it again.

"Should I phone them?" Krystyna asked, tentatively.

"No, no, er, no, it's best if I do it," Vince said. "Why don't you get going? It's been a busy day and I'm not staying late tonight."

"But I should work until five," Krystyna replied.

Vince sat back and gave a grandiose sweep of an arm. "No, you get along. I'm going to ring these cretins and give them a piece of my mind. Anyway, you don't want to hear me when I'm angry."

"Fine," Krystyna said. "I'll go then. See you in the morning."

"Tomorrow," Vince said, "I'll show you that new spreadsheet that I've designed."

Krystyna gave him a slightly sickly smile and walked slowly to the front door. She closed it quietly behind her and leant back against the wall for a second. Then she started to giggle. She found that she couldn't stop giggling and had to grasp hold of a drainpipe to support herself. Her eyes had become moist and she felt tears beginning to trickle over her cheeks. She wiped her eyes, took a deep breath of air and walked towards her bus stop.

Chapter 2

Sean Monaghan was in the kitchen, making tea, when the telephone rang. His partner, Carol Whelan, who was sitting in the living room doing the crossword in *The Guardian*, called, "Let it go," which was Carol-speak for "leave it to the answerphone". Sean, though, had already picked up the phone in the kitchen.

Carol, realising that the call was for Sean, took little notice of the conversation as she battled with a 15-letter anagram. She had worked it out just as Sean appeared with the tea. "Shopping centres," she said.

Sean looked puzzled for a second as he sat down and then looked at the crossword she was holding. "Oh, I see," he said. "You're clever."

"I know," Carol said. "Who was that?"

"You'll never guess," Sean said.

Carol considered the possibilities and opted for one of the more obvious. "Right, don't tell me. Some guy with an Indian accent calling himself Jimmy McTavish?"

"Not this time," Sean said.

"Last two I've had called themselves Paul and John. Next one, I'm going to insist on speaking to George or Ringo."

"It wasn't pop royalty, but it *was* royalty. That was The King."

Now it was Carol that looked baffled, but only for a moment. "Oh God," she said, "what did that poltroon want?"

Sean hesitated for a second. "Only wants me to go and work for him."

Carol snorted derisively. "Hope you told him to shove it up..."

"I said I'd think about it."

"You were always more polite than me."

Sean took a sip of tea, more to give himself a moment to think than anything else. "I could, though. Just for a few months."

Carol looked hard at him and said, "Did you put something in that tea?"

"We could use the money, though. Have another little trip to Eastern Europe."

"Well, yeah, I'm all for that. But Vince?"

"Why not? He'll be out and about most of the time, hobnobbing and getting free lunches. I'll be sitting in the office doing not much. Listening to the odd golf bore, knocking up a few spreadsheets, okay hundreds of spreadsheets, but it's not exactly stressful."

"You do all the work and he gets all the credit."

"That won't change, just we won't be civil servants this time."

Carol made a face. "Yeah, he's not civil and you'll be the servant. He won't pay you much, either," she said.

Sean nodded. "Of course, but even the great VK has to pay the minimum wage. Why not? Just until you finish your doctorate."

"I suppose so," Carol said, sounding a long distance from convinced.

"Anyway," Sean added, "I can tell you all of the improbable things he claims to have done. All the new improbable things."

Carol looked more enthused about this prospect. "Climbed Everest blindfold," she suggested.

"And handcuffed. Why make it easy?"

"Turned down the coach's job at Barcelona."

"Only after he'd turned down Real Madrid and Bayern Munich."

They sat and pondered for a while over Vince's likely achievements. Carol asked "How many staff has he got now?"

Sean said, "A couple of young women. He was drooling on about this Polish girl he's got there."

Carol shuddered. "Creepy. He's always got some girl he drools over."

"All the time," Sean agreed. "Always about half his age, as well. Not that he ever does anything, but it is creepy. Sounds like he's smitten with this one, though. Kept telling me how good her English is."

"More than you can say for his," Carol said. "Has he really got so many customers that he needs extra staff?"

Sean shrugged. "Probably not," he said, "but he seems to have customers, at least. You know what he's like, though. He has to be a manager. He has to be in charge. He has to have staff. He's a control freak."

"I know," Carol said. "That's why I'm not sure it's a good idea."

"Vince doesn't scare me," Sean said. "He just makes me laugh. Not that he means to, obviously."

"Go on then, Sergeant Wilson. Go and tell Captain Mainwaring that you'll accept." Carol folded her paper and swatted Sean gently on the head with it. "Just promise me one thing – you won't put this on your CV. There's only so much humiliation a person can take."

Sean grimaced. "Dear God, no. I'm not giving anybody a CV that says 'Golf King'. I'll put something like 'Drug Dealer'."

Chapter 3

Vince Kingmyle followed the same routine each morning. His wife, Valerie, got up precisely half an hour before Vince, who then rose, showered, dressed and came downstairs for the breakfast that she had prepared. Afterwards, he drove her to the department store where she worked before going to his own office.

As he waited for Valerie this particular morning, Vince checked his appearance in the living-room mirror. He spotted an annoying tuft of hair sticking up just above his right ear, licked his fingers and smoothed it down. The dark hair at the side and back of his head was the only hair he possessed and it served to give him a slightly monkish appearance, set against the shiny dome of his head.

He tightened his tie and surveyed his reflection with satisfaction. He looked the part of the successful businessman, he felt, as he opened his briefcase. Into it, he placed his lunchbox, packed by Valerie the previous evening, and his copy of *The Sun*.

The sight of the paper made him think of Sean Monaghan, with whom he was soon to be reacquainted. Sean never bothered to disguise his contempt for that newspaper. Vince could not understand this, but there were lots of things he didn't understand about Sean. When he'd been Sean's boss in the Civil Service, he had constantly encouraged him to apply for promotion. Vince could not understand why Sean, who had a degree, was apparently content to do the work of a mere clerical officer.

Nor could Vince comprehend Sean's complete lack of interest in the work he did. It wasn't as if he was bad at his job – far from it – but he seemed to regard it with utter indifference. He put it down to Sean's artistic temperament and the fact that he had studied English Literature. Vince could see no point in that.

What was anybody going to learn about life by reading a load of old books that were of no relevance in the modern world.

Then there was art. Vince hated art. What was the use of it? Sean, though, kept going to all these strange places and when he came back, all he could talk about was art galleries, museums, architecture and boring rubbish like that. When Vince went on holiday, he went to enjoy himself. He, Valerie and their daughter Victoria went to Florida every year. Vince played golf for three weeks and the women did whatever it was that women do. Shopping, mostly, he assumed.

He was not, he prided himself, a creature of habit, though. Now and then they went to Tenerife, and one year they had even gone to the Algarve. The golf courses had been good there and Vince wondered if another visit was in order soon.

Sean, though, went to all these grim and dingy places in Eastern Europe, yet would come back enthusing about them. Romania, Bosnia, Croatia, Ukraine, Lithuania, Poland and all sorts of dumps that didn't have a single golf course between them. Where, Vince wondered, was the fun in that?

Charitably, he came to the conclusion that it wasn't all Sean's fault. Most of it was down to that bloody woman he lived with, what was her name? Carol, that was it. Art historian, she called herself. Vince could think of plenty of other names for her.

Yes, thought Vince, take away her influence and Sean was a decent fellow. He couldn't be that bad; after all, he liked football and even seemed to have a decent knowledge of the game. Of course, he could never have the same level of expertise as someone who had played at the kind of level Vince had, but he knew his stuff. Even so, Sean would start going on about these weird foreign coaches like Herrera and Lobanovskiy.

Still, if there was someone who could sort out the mess that Vince's IT system had got into, it was Sean. The man had a very logical approach, Vince conceded, and that was exactly what was required. He needed somebody to come in and make the place run smoothly. True, Krystyna was very good and the clients liked her. It was those dark eyes and the husky Polish accent. Anne wasn't exactly the brightest firework in the box, but she did what she was told and Vince liked that. Sean had a maverick streak, but Vince knew how to handle him. After all, he'd done it for eight years or so before, so he could do it now.

Vince picked up his briefcase as he heard Valerie coming down the stairs. She had been sceptical of his Golf King venture, as had others, but he had proved them all wrong. It had been a brilliant idea, he considered, on his part.

In fact, the idea had come about when Vince had been talking to a colleague about golf. Vince often talked about golf. The colleague had noted that an increasingly large number of tourists were coming to Scotland to play. "Someone could cash in there," he'd said. And so Vince had.

"She still in bed?" Vince asked his wife.

"Fast asleep," Valerie replied.

Vince shook his head. His daughter had recently left school and seemed to think she was entitled to stay in bed all day. That would change, he resolved, but for now, he had lots of work to do.

Chapter 4

When Sean boarded the eight o'clock train to Edinburgh on a Monday morning, he remembered why he'd left his Civil Service job in the first place. He saw the same – and just as unhappy – faces that he'd seen every day. He saw, with distaste, the people who insisted on sitting on the outside seats, even when the train was crowded, and who only moved with huge reluctance and even huger sighs if you asked them if you could sit down. He saw the increasingly vast rucksacks that people insisted on carrying every day. What on earth did they put in these things, he wondered.

He buried himself in his copy of *The Guardian* and consoled himself with the thought that he wouldn't be doing this for long. It might be amusing for a while, but there was only so much of Vince that one could take.

Haymarket station was as busy as ever at quarter to nine in the morning. Vince had told him to come at ten o'clock and Sean suspected, correctly, that this was because Vince never got to the office before half past nine. He went to a coffee shop and drank a leisurely macchiato before he strolled to the office.

The office was in one of the Georgian terraces in Edinburgh's New Town and Sean wondered how much the rent was. Either Vince was making a go of this business or he was living beyond his means. Not that he cared a great deal as long as he got paid. The building was shared with a few other businesses and Sean surveyed the 'Golf King' plaque on the outside of the building before he went in.

Vince greeted him like an old friend; Vince had always considered Sean to be a friend, though the feeling was hardly mutual. Vince introduced him to Krystyna and Anne, as well as the desk he would be using. Sean got the impression that Krystyna's greeting was a little frosty, but some people were naturally reserved and he didn't give it much thought.

"Get yourself a cup of tea and we'll have a chat," said Vince.

Sean boiled the kettle and made the tea with one of the cheap, bulk-buy teabags that were by the kettle, making a mental note to go to a shop at lunchtime to buy some decent tea. By the time he'd made something vaguely drinkable, Vince was standing beside him with an A4 pad in his hand.

After a few pleasantries, Vince got down to business. "We're taking off," he said. "That's why I called you. I'm so busy with meeting people and being out of the office so much, I need someone to keep things organised. The girls do a grand job, but they're not so great on IT stuff. I want you to get the IT system organised."

Sean took a mouthful of insipid tea and asked, "You've got plenty of customers, then?"

Vince nodded. "Loads," he said. "Lots from England and Ireland. Had some Germans as well and I'm meeting some Japanese people tomorrow. I've got some Americans interested as well. I want to crack the American market."

"I see," Sean said, calmly, as he saw the old evangelical zeal rising in his old boss. "So what's my role? Do you want me to just do the IT or do I have to do other stuff?"

"We'll see how it develops," said Vince. "You don't play golf, do you?"

"No," said Sean.

"Pity," Vince said. "It's a good way of getting to know people. I do a lot of networking and a round of golf is good business practice. You could learn. You've played cricket, so I'm sure you could manage golf."

Sean shook his head. "Don't like the game," he said.

"Oh well, never mind," said Vince. "You stick to the IT and admin for now. The girls can answer the phones and speak to clients. You don't need to worry about being on the phone all the time."

"Good," said Sean, with evident relief.

"What I'd like to start with is the spreadsheets," said Vince, producing several sheets of paper covered in notes. "They need a bit of, er, tidying up. I want you to look at all of them and try to rationalise things a bit. We've got too much duplication of data."

"How many spreadsheets have you got?" asked Sean, with some trepidation.

"About eighty or so," said Vince. Receiving no reply, he added, "It might take you a while."

"I'd imagine so," Sean said, non-committally.

"I've listed most of the stuff here," Vince said, spreading out his notes across the table. "What we've got, what we haven't got, what we need, what we don't need. I'd like you to go through all of them and make something more manageable."

Sean glanced at the mass of hieroglyphs in front of him and said, "Why don't we have a spreadsheet that tells us what all these spreadsheets are?"

Vince stared at him for a moment and said, "That's it. You've got it. Brilliant idea – set one up."

Chapter 5

Sean worked at the spreadsheets for the rest of the day and into the following morning. Vince, who had arrived at the relatively early time of half past nine, busied himself at his computer and sent his team an email, drafted in his own, idiosyncratic fashion. It read:

I have, made the decision to create a new spreadsheet which will contain information regarding all of the spreadsheets that we currently use. Sean will, compile this spreadsheet and when he has completed the task I will, give a presentation to explain how we will use it and the other spreadsheets that we have on the system.

Vince Kingmyle
Managing Director
Golf King Ltd

Aside from a slight grimace, Sean showed no reaction. He'd read plenty of emails of this nature before and he ploughed on with the spreadsheet project. Vince would be going to his meeting soon and he'd get a bit of peace. Anne never had much to say and Krystyna seemed to have taken a dislike to him, so he didn't expect much interruption.

It came as a surprise then, when Vince asked him to come to the meeting with the Japanese clients. Sean's initial thought was that he'd rather stay put, but he'd been staring at spreadsheets for the best part of a day and decided that getting out of the office for a while would not be the worst idea.

As they walked to Vince's car, Vince said that the meeting was at a hotel in the West End. Sean couldn't quite fathom why the booking couldn't simply be done over the telephone, but assumed that sitting around in a swanky hotel was part of

Vince's desire to look important. Besides, there was a book he wanted to buy and once the meeting had finished, he could walk around the corner to Waterstone's bookshop.

On the way, Vince gave him the lowdown. There was a party of twelve and they wanted to play not just one, but four golf courses. He was clearly excited by the prospect of the bookings. "We'll be big in Japan," he enthused.

Vince went to reception and was directed to the meeting room that he had booked. The two Japanese had not yet arrived at the hotel, but they were there within a few minutes. A waitress arrived, offering tea and coffee. Sean and the two Japanese, both middle-aged businessmen, took tea. Vince, who drank neither tea nor coffee, had a bottle of mineral water. The waitress also left a plate of biscuits.

It was all fairly straightforward, as Sean had suspected. There was really no need for this hotel stuff, he thought. If Vince had wanted to impress them, why not just use his own office? It was in a smart enough location. He could have understood it if the office had been in a rundown part of Leith, Granton, Sighthill or somewhere like that, but it wasn't.

There was, one of the Japanese said, a minor problem.

"What's that?" asked Vince.

"We have no clubs," the man replied.

"Not a problem," Vince said. "You can hire clubs."

"From where?" the man asked.

"From me," Vince told him. "I can arrange all that." He gave a little smirk and adopted an unconvincing Far East accent. "I am the Loan Arranger," he announced.

The Japanese stared at him as if fulfilling some contractual obligation to remain inscrutable. Sean closed his eyes and wished he were somewhere else, preferably on another continent.

After the Japanese had left, Vince, full of self-satisfaction, noticed that the biscuits had remained untouched. He unfolded a serviette, tipped the biscuits onto it, wrapped them and slipped them into his pocket. "No point in wasting things," he said, cheerfully.

"Not coming back with me, Tonto?" asked Vince as they left the hotel.

"Just popping into town," said Sean, who had planned to anyway, but was looking forward to getting away from Vince for a while. He decided to phone Carol to relay the dire events of the morning. Her reaction was what he expected.

"God," she said, "he's lucky you're a pacifist. I'd have brained him."

"Wouldn't that require the presence of a brain?" Sean asked.

"Fair point," Carol conceded.

Sean considered things for a moment and then said, "If he gets any Chinese clients, I'm going as Elvis."

"Why?" Carol asked, already dreading the response.

"Because it's yuan for the money," Sean said. He only avoided a perforated eardrum by quickly removing the phone from the proximity of that organ.

Chapter 6

So things went on. Vince continued to drum up custom, at least in his own mind, by spending more and more time on the golf course. Anne continued to come in and do very little, say very little, then go home. Krystyna continued to answer the phone, make bookings and do a lot of typing. Sean continued his ascent of the spreadsheet mountain and even found time to write a couple of database applications.

One Friday lunchtime, Sean was eating a sandwich and reading the paper when the doorbell rang. Krystyna jumped up to answer the door and Sean continued reading. He heard Krystyna say, "He's just gone out to the shops. You can wait for him here."

"Hello there," said a voice from across the desk. Sean looked up. It was Stuart Webster, who had been a colleague in the Civil Service. "Didn't know you were working for Vince," he said.

"Not long started," said Sean, who didn't know Stuart particularly well. He did, though, know that Stuart was a golfing partner of Vince's and, like Vince, a Hearts fan.

They had a brief exchange of pleasantries before Vince returned carrying a plastic cup of soup and a copy of the *Edinburgh Evening News*. He did this every lunchtime when he was at the office. It transpired that Vince and Stuart were going to play golf in the afternoon, though Vince had neglected to mention that he was leaving early.

Sean finished his lunch and went back to the database he was toying with. For the best part of two hours, Vince and Stuart sat there talking about football. Not that Stuart actually said very much. Sean tried to concentrate on his work and blot out the continuous drone that was emanating from across the desk.

He was only partially successful. He discerned that Stuart had not made it to the last game at Tynecastle and Vince was giving him the full story. In fact, it was something more than the full story. Sean caught snippets of the monologue.

"They've got no leader, nobody who can organise...we need a centre forward who can hold the ball up...the midfield and defence are too far apart...if you're playing a lone striker, he has to run the channels...you need midfield runners from deep...the full backs can't defend...the goalkeeper doesn't command his box...people don't understand...I've played at the highest level..."

After an hour, Sean went and made a cup of tea. He took his time about it and prayed that it was time for Vince to go to his golf. It was a forlorn hope and when he got back to his desk, the one-man show was still in full flow. He wondered why Stuart put up with it.

Vince had played 90 minutes, plus a considerable amount of injury time. Eventually, he came to the end and stood up. "Okay, see you on Monday," he said, and the pair departed for the golf course.

Sean exhaled heavily and muttered, "It would have been quicker to show a video of the match." He hadn't really been addressing it to anyone in particular and with Anne having a day off, there was only Krystyna left in the office. To his surprise, she laughed loudly.

"He does go on, doesn't he?" she said.

"Just a bit," Sean agreed.

Krystyna got up and walked round to Sean's desk. She sat down and said, "And I thought you were of friend of Vince."

Sean shook his head. "Not me. You've got the wrong man."

Krystyna smiled and said, "He thinks you are his friend."

"Vince thinks a lot of strange things," Sean replied.

"But you know him from before," said Krystyna.

"Yes," Sean said. "That's undeniable. But friends we are not."

"Why did you come to work for him?" Krystyna asked.

"I was a bit hard up," Sean admitted.

Krystyna smiled again and said, "Yes, me too. And I need to

pay for my Open University course."

"Which one are you doing?" Sean asked.

"I am doing twentieth-century literature."

Sean laughed. Krystyna frowned and he quickly explained, "I looked at that when I did my OU degree. It looked a bit difficult to me. I did the nineteenth-century novel course instead."

"How funny," Krystyna said. "I looked at that course and thought it might be difficult. But maybe I could do that next year."

"I didn't fancy the twentieth-century literature course and it's my first language," Sean said. "I'm not being patronising, but that's really impressive. I wouldn't get very far if I had to do a course in Polish."

"Yes, but I learned English from very early in school," said Krystyna. "It's not such a hard language. Polish is very difficult. Well, not for Poles, but for anybody else."

"I can say 'dzien dobry' and 'do widzenia'," Sean offered.

"Very good," Krystyna said approvingly.

"But they're easy because they're almost the same in lots of languages. Russian, Croatian, Slavic languages. I can probably say 'good afternoon' in about twenty languages, but I can't speak any of them."

Krystyna smiled and said, "But at least you can speak your own language correctly, which is more than Vince."

Sean nodded in emphatic agreement. "I know," he said. "His emails are embarrassing sometimes."

"Only sometimes?" Krystyna said. "He gives me letters to send to clients and I have to rewrite them. Isn't it so silly? I am Polish and I have to correct letters in English."

They had given up on the idea of doing any more work today. Krystyna told Sean that Vince regarded her Open University course as pointless.

"Vince doesn't like anything that even hints at academia," Sean said. "He had the same attitude to my course. Same with anything remotely arty. That's taboo, as well. He is, in a fact, a complete philistine. Do you know, he actually hoped his daughter would fail her exams so she wouldn't be tempted to go to university."

Krystyna wasn't sure whether to laugh or be outraged. "He told me she had left school, but he said nothing about her grades, so I thought it best not to ask. I know he was complaining about her lying in bed half the day and not getting a job."

"She could always start a band," Sean said. Krystyna looked suitably puzzled. He said, "Well, she was named after a Spice Girl."

Krystyna looked at him with a mixture of amusement and disbelief. "Please tell me you are joking," she said.

Sean shook his head. "No, I'm deadly serious. She was born in 1996. Height of Spice Girl mania. And of course he had to give her a name that started with V. There has to be a 'V' everywhere with Vince."

Now it was Krystyna who shook her head. "I know," she said morosely. Then she grinned and said, "I would give him a 'V', though." She put up two fingers and thrust them defiantly in the direction of Vince's desk.

Chapter 7

The great campaign to attract American custom continued. Vince was a great admirer of all things American and had, at one stage, been certain that he was on the verge of retiring to Florida. The department for which he had worked had offered a number of early-retirement packages. Information had been published explaining the terms and conditions, with useful calculators to enable people to gauge their own, individual situations. Vince had spent an entire morning utilising an assortment of spreadsheets and calculators before arriving at a figure.

Unfortunately for him, the figure he arrived at was an exact multiple of ten of the real figure. It had only been when he'd started looking at American property websites that some spoilsport had pointed out to him that it was perhaps a little unlikely that the UK government would be offering retirement packages worth around half a million pounds to low-ranking managerial staff.

Vince, though, prided himself on his resilience and still had the vision of a Florida future. Scotland had some lovely golf courses, but just didn't have the weather. Still, those very golf courses would be his ticket to a sunnier climate and he thought it rather neat that his dream of escaping Scotland for America should be provided by Americans escaping their own country for the delights of Scottish golf courses.

There was a long way to go, that much he knew. Nonetheless, the signing of the first American contract was a serious cause for celebration. He was feeling uncommonly magnanimous when he sent his three members of staff an email inviting them to join him for drink at his West End club on a Friday afternoon.

Vince had joined this particular club a couple of years ago and had been especially pleased that one of the witnesses who'd signed his application was a retired army officer. Vince liked the prestige attached to this club, which was one of many he had joined. He was also a member of his local Rotary Club and had membership of several golf clubs. To Vince, status was everything and the more memberships he acquired, the higher his standing in society.

Sean, on the other hand, took the Groucho Marx view that he would not want to be a member of any club that would have him as a member. He was tempted to turn down the invitation, but getting a free drink out of Vince seemed about as plausible as Berwick Rangers winning the Champions League, so he thought he may as well go and witness such a notable occasion.

Feeling that he might need some support, Sean had enlisted the one-woman crack regiment otherwise known as Carol. She was in town anyway and Sean walked along to Waterstone's on Princes Street, where she was collecting a book that she had ordered for her course.

It would be an exaggeration to say that Carol was overcome with excitement at the prospect, but she imagined that they would not be staying very long and that they could have a couple more drinks in more amenable surroundings. With that in mind, she suggested they repair to the Guildford Arms before they caught the train home. Sean gave unreserved approval to the idea and they walked to the club, where no doubt Vince was holding court.

Krystyna and Anne had gone with their boss and when Sean and Carol arrived, Krystyna spotted them and waved. Sean waved back and as Vince got up, gave Carol a nudge. To his relief, he'd noticed a pair of hand pumps on the bar. "Real beer, thank God for that," he said.

Vince came over. "What can I get you?" he asked.

"Definitely a pint of Deuchars IPA for me," Sean said.

Carol added, "And me as well."

Vince glanced at the barman, who was serving the only other customer at the bar. "It'll have to be a half," he told Carol.

She stared at him and said, "I don't want a half. I want a pint."

Vince leant towards her and said quietly, "They don't, er, serve pints to ladies."

He was spared a response from Carol, but unluckily for Vince, the barman was a man blessed with an acute sense of hearing.

"Yes, we do," said the barman. "We serve anybody what they like, as long as they're sober. And this lady looks perfectly sober to me."

Vince gave the barman a look that should, by rights, have made the beer curdle. As a counterbalance, the barman received a smile from Carol and drew two pints of IPA. Vince told him to put it on his account. He'd have liked to have told him something else, but managed to restrain himself, for once.

Once everyone had sat down, Vince looked at the Waterstone's bag and said to Sean, "More books? You're turning into a doddery old fuddy-duddy."

Carol put her pint down and regarded Vince with an expression of amused contempt. "That's a proven theory, is it? Only old people read books?"

Vince, slightly taken aback by Carol's warning shot, said, "No, I didn't say that. It's just that it doesn't seem healthy to spend all your time reading books. People who are busy and active don't sit around getting bored."

"There's nothing boring about reading," Carol said. "It's educational, informative, thought-provoking and it broadens the mind. Maybe you should try it one day." Across the table, Krystyna tried not to grin too hard.

Vince had met Carol before and knew it was not advisable to push his luck. He found refuge in a weak bladder and went to the toilet. As he walked, he could swear that he felt a cold tingle in his spine from Carol's piercing grey eyes.

Carol took a rewarding sip of her beer and said, "Vince is so well read that he thinks *Moby Dick* is a sexually transmitted disease."

Sean, who was used to Carol's one-liners, merely smiled indulgently. Anne stared blankly across the room. Unfortunately, Krystyna was in the process of taking a mouthful of her drink and nearly choked herself. She had only just recovered from her coughing fit when Vince returned.

It couldn't last, though, and Krystyna burst into a fit of giggles. Vince, in a rare moment of perception, feared the joke might be on him and asked her to share it. Carol came to the rescue.

"It was my fault," she said, which was true. "It was a joke I heard at the OU. How many Edinburgh University rugby players does it take to change a light bulb?" Receiving no offers, she said, "Sixteen. One to hold the bulb in the air and the other fifteen to keep drinking until the room starts spinning round."

Krystyna started laughing again and Vince frowned. Keen to change the subject, he raised his slimline soft drink and said, "To our first American booking."

This, at least, was reasonably uncontentious and it gave Vince the opportunity to talk about two subjects he loved, golf and himself. Not that any of the others were in the least interested in the game. Vince, however, was not to be deterred by such minor details. He regaled the company with an impressive list of courses he had played; St Andrew's, Carnoustie, Troon, Gleneagles, Muirfield and many, many more.

When he reached the list of English courses, Carol slapped a hand to her knee and said, "Oh, that's just reminded me. I need to go down to Guildford soon." She gave Sean a meaningful look, one that was not lost on him.

The prompt was a useful one and they finished their drinks. Vince said, "Going so soon?" though he felt a wave of relief that he'd be seeing the back of Carol. He didn't know what Sean saw in the woman. She was, he had to admit, quite attractive, with her dark brown, bobbed hair and pleasing figure, but she had a tongue like barbed wire. Not only that, she was left-wing, feminist and all kinds of other weird things that Vince did not and could not understand.

"Straight to Guildford, now," Carol whispered in Sean's ear as they left the club.

Back at the club, Anne needed to get moving and Krystyna certainly saw no reason to stay. If Vince was put out by the early break-up of his party, he showed no signs of it. "That was a good evening," he said with satisfaction. "We must do it again sometime."

"Yes, one day," said Krystyna politely, while hoping that day would be some time after she had left the employ of Golf King. Vince, taking encouragement from this, asked her if she would like to move on somewhere else.

"No, thank you, I am very busy," Krystyna lied. She had nothing whatsoever to do and began to wish that she had gone with Sean and Carol. Even so, an evening sitting in front of the television by herself had considerable appeal when one considered the alternative.

"Never mind," said Vince jovially. He watched Krystyna and Anne leave, then picked up his empty glass to return it to the bar. Then he remembered the barman and left the glass on the table. The fool could come and get it himself.

Chapter 8

Still on a considerable high from the inaugural American booking, Vince received a further boost the following week. The 'King of Swing' shirts arrived on Wednesday, this time bearing the correct text. Vince immediately donned one and wore it for the remainder of the day.

Not that it was a long day, at least for Vince. Having arrived in the office after ten o'clock, he was so overcome by the excitement that he decided to finish his day just after Anne had departed at half past three.

Before he left, he ensured that his remaining troops were fully occupied. Krystyna had a batch of letters to keep her busy and Vince asked Sean what he was working on.

"I'm doing that data-entry application that you wanted," Sean said.

"When do you think it'll be ready?" Vince wanted to know.

"Hard to say," Sean said vaguely. "It's a bit of a tricky one. The only way you can do it is using three-dimensional tables and they're notoriously awkward. And we'll need to test it with realistic data. I can create—"

He got no further. "Fine, fine," said Vince, with a dismissive wave of his hand. "Let me know when it's ready. I have to go. So much to do."

"So much golf to play, so little time," said Sean, but only after the front door had closed. Krystyna sniggered and peeped out of the window. She watched Vince get into his car and drive off, then came round to Sean's desk.

"I have to tell you this," she said, almost whispering, as though Vince had somehow retained a hearing presence in his office. She told Sean about the first consignment of the 'King of Swing', or more correctly, 'King of Swine', shirts that had arrived.

When Sean had stopped laughing – and it took some time – he asked if there were any of the original batch left.

Krystyna shook her head. "No, he sent them all back."

"Damn," said Sean, with genuine feeling. "I'd have paid good money for one of those."

"One of those, yes, one of these, no," Krystyna said, jabbing one of the boxes with her foot.

"No chance,'" Sean agreed.

"How is Carol?" Krystyna asked. There was little more to say about polo shirts.

"Fine," Sean said.

"Good." Krystyna smiled and said, "She gave Vince a hard time. I like Carol."

Sean smiled back and said, "So do I."

Krystyna laughed and said, "I should hope so. I think that Vince does not like Carol, though."

"Vince definitely does not like Carol. Not one little bit," said Sean, with a certain amount of pride in his voice.

Krystyna, once more in conspiratorial tones, told Sean about Vince's Friday-night offer. Sensing her understandable unease, Sean told her that Vince had something of a track record in regard of younger women. "He doesn't do anything, though," he added, as Krystyna looked even more concerned. "He's just smarmy. I think he sees himself as some sort of irresistible James Bond type, but he'd never dare try anything."

"He'd better not," Krystyna said, "or I will bring in some Polish black bread and smash him over the head with it."

Sean laughed. "You could force him to drink some Polish porter. That would knock him out."

Now Krystyna laughed. "That would knock anybody out. You have tried it?"

Sean nodded. "In Krakow. Just a small bottle and only one. It think it was 9.3 percent."

They sat and talked about Krakow and Poland for a while,

then Sean said, "I don't see any point in hanging around here. There's no way that Vince is going to come back."

Krystyna agreed and switched off her computer and put on her jacket. Sean was still tidying things away when she said, "One last question." Sean looked up and she said, "Are you really writing something that has a three-dimensional table?"

Sean shook his head. "No, I'm not and I've no intention of writing anything with a three-dimensional table in it. Actually, I finished it earlier, but I wasn't going to tell Vince that or he'd have given me some other pointless piece of rubbish to do. I just came up with the first piece of bull I could think of."

"That's exactly what I thought," said Krystyna. She said goodnight and left.

Chapter 9

Vince, meanwhile, had played a round of golf. Having telephoned his wife to tell her precisely when he would be home, he arrived to find his dinner waiting for him.

He was disappointed that Valerie had failed to notice his shirt and felt obliged to point it out to her. She did manage a "very nice", but that was all and he felt that this showed a lack of understanding. Then again, he considered, what could women be expected to know about either business or golf?

"Where's Victoria?" he asked when he had finished his meal. "She can't still be in bed."

"Of course she isn't," said Valerie. "This should cheer you up. She's got a job."

Vince stared at his wife for a moment. "When did this happen?" he asked.

"Just today. One of her friends has a brother who runs a pub and offered her a job in the bar."

"Why was I not informed of this?" demanded Vince.

"Because it's only just happened. They were a bit short of staff and asked if she could start today."

Vince sighed. While he didn't want his daughter lying in bed all the time, he wasn't entirely sure this he wanted her being a barmaid, either, a sentiment he made known to his wife.

"She's got to start somewhere," said Valerie, with admirable practicality. "She won't be doing it for long and it gives her the chance to see what it's like to work for a living."

"She's not going to make much of a living working in a pub," said Vince.

"No, but she'll move on to something else soon enough," Valerie said.

Vince had a sudden thought. "What about your place? Don't they have vacancies? I'd prefer her to work in a reputable store than some seedy pub."

"It's not a seedy pub," Valerie protested. "It's one of those brand-new places down in Leith, you know, by the shore. They're all smart and yuppie down there now."

Vince pulled a face. "Great," he said. "Leith yuppies and a bunch of Hibbees for company. What more could you want?"

Valerie gave a rather wan smile and then addressed Vince's original question. "There's not much going at our place, unless she wants a cleaning job. Things have changed, you don't get the kind of shop floor to management ladder you used to have years ago. They want graduate entrants now and unless she goes back and studies again, she won't get anywhere with that."

What Valerie had just done, in effect, was to flutter a very scarlet piece of material in front of the bull that was sitting in the living room. Vince's nostrils flared and he prepared his charge.

"Graduates," he said, loading the word with as much contempt as he could muster. "What do they know about anything? They've never experienced life. They don't have any understanding of what it's like, they don't know the business. It was the same in the Civil Service. It was fine in the days when people started at the bottom. You'd go in as a clerical assistant and work your way up. If you were any good, you became a manager and there were people at the top – right at the top, I mean – who started as clerical assistants. That's the way to run an organisation, not bringing in a load of namby-pamby students who don't know anything."

Valerie, who worked with some graduate trainees and found them very nice people, knew better than to attempt anything resembling a contrary view. Meanwhile, the bull continued to rage.

"Look at what happened to me. Joined from school as a clerical assistant, promoted to clerical officer in five years and then another promotion ten years after that. Then what? Nothing. The road is blocked by a bunch of spotty students who know sweet FA. I have all this experience, but do they want that? No, they don't. I'm the best manager, but does that mean anything. No, it does not. Do you know how many of my staff got promoted? I'll tell you exactly – twenty-three. And why was that? Because I was the best manager, I knew how to get the best out of people. Figures proved that I was the best manager. Everybody knew that I was the best manager. Does that do me any good? No. Does that count for anything? No. Because it's all about how good a degree you've got, not what you know about the job or how to manage people."

There was a silence. Vince had finished and Valerie waited for a second or two to see if there was to be an aftershock after the main eruption. Satisfied that Vince had blown himself out, she slowly got up from the sofa and went to the kitchen to do the washing up.

Vince looked at the time and contemplated waiting up for Victoria to come home. He suspected that it would be after midnight, though, and he was feeling tired. He wasn't too thrilled that his daughter had embarked on a career as a barmaid, but at least it ensured that she got out of bed occasionally and it might instil a little discipline. Anyway, as Valerie had said, she wasn't likely to be doing the job for very long. He wondered whether he might be able to find a job for her at Golf King, but couldn't really see what she could do. Valerie had mentioned the possibility when Vince had talked about recruiting someone, but he'd needed somebody who knew IT and while Victoria knew her way around Facebook and Twitter, she wasn't going to be much help when it came to databases and spreadsheets.

He decided against sitting around until she came home. He went up for a shower and carefully laid his 'King of Swing' shirt into the laundry basket in the bathroom. He gave a nod of satisfaction. The printing accident was completely forgotten now.

Chapter 10

Krystyna was the only person in the office when the phone rang at quarter to five on a Thursday afternoon. As she was just about ready to leave, she considered ignoring it, but picked it up and found herself speaking to Carol Whelan.

Carol explained that she had come into Edinburgh and been detained rather longer than she had expected. She thought that Sean might fancy going for a drink. Krystyna told her that Vince had sent Sean on some mission and she wasn't sure when he would be back. She did, though, know that Sean would be returning to the office.

Carol had an idea. "Well, I'm going for a drink," she said. "Would you like to come?"

Krystyna had been intending to work on an Open University assignment that evening, but this seemed more appealing. The OU, she decided, could wait.

"Do you know the Cumberland Bar?" Carol asked. Krystyna did. "Okay, meet me there in twenty minutes, half an hour. Could you leave a note on Sean's desk and let him know where we are?"

Krystyna did that and twenty minutes later, she was sitting with a drink in front of her. She was pleased to have a chance to talk to Carol. There hadn't been much opportunity that night in the club, particularly with Vince's presence looming over proceedings.

They were enjoying a chat about art and literature when Sean turned up. He had the appearance of someone to whom firearms should not be issued at any cost.

"What's up, duck?" asked Carol.

Sean shook his head. "Tell you in a minute," he said. "I need a drink."

He brought back three drinks from the bar and sat down.

"Have a guess," he said.

"VK?" suggested Carol.

"Correct," Sean said. He took a swig of beer and said, "First, he sends me all the way out to Corstorphine to see a man who wasn't there and to collect a document that didn't exist." He fortified himself with another gulp and went on, "Now he wants me to meet him tomorrow at some golf course in the middle of nowhere."

"Where's nowhere?" asked Carol.

"Fife," said Sean.

"We live in Fife," said Carol.

"I'd spotted that," Sean said. "But we don't live in Elie, do we?"

"Not the last time I checked," Carol confirmed.

"He seems to think he's doing me a favour. He left me an email saying to meet him at this golf club and how it would save me coming into Edinburgh. And how it would save me a train fare. Well, it doesn't. I've got a season ticket, plus I'll have to get to Kirkcaldy and get a bus from there. All at extra expense. And I'll guarantee that he won't refund me."

"Why won't he give you a lift?" Carol asked.

"God knows. He's going to have to drive past our house, virtually." Sean gazed moodily at his diminishing pint and looked up. "There's one bright side," he said. "At least I won't have to sit in a car and listen to him talking."

"Maybe he will have one of his days when he does not talk," Krystyna said. "Sometimes, he never stops talking. Other days, he never speaks."

"I prefer the other days," said Sean.

"Vince is such a misanthrope that he doesn't even talk to himself," Carol said.

"Except when he's looking in the mirror," Sean said.

Krystyna smiled, then frowned. "One thing maybe you can explain," she said. "When he is talking about football to people, he is always saying about how he played at the 'highest level'. What does he mean? Who did he play for?"

Carol had an answer to that one. "He went to Bolivia by mistake once and played football on the top of a multi-story car park in La Paz."

Krystyna laughed and said, "Seriously, though, did he ever play as a professional?"

"Not a chance," Sean said. "Mind you, I wouldn't mind having a fiver for every time I've heard that 'I played at the highest level' line. My theory is that he went along to one of those open days that football clubs have for schools and he reckons that counts as playing for them. He still plays football and I was talking to another chap that's played with him and he reckons Vince is rubbish. He does a lot of shouting and pointing, but he isn't actually any good. If you'd played professionally, even if it was only non-league stuff, you'd stand out in the sort of kick-about games he plays. Even at fifty, you'd still have the ball control and passing, even if you didn't have any pace."

"I bet he gets very upset if he does not win," Krystyna said.

"Guarantee it," Sean agreed. "He's like an oversized baby. Something doesn't go his way and he starts screaming."

Three drinks later and Carol looked at her watch. "Do you realise," she said, "that we have spent the last two and a bit hours talking about Vince Kingmyle?"

Sean and Krystyna looked suitably horrified. "I'll have to see how red his ears look tomorrow," Sean said. He finished his drink and suddenly felt very tired. He felt like a man who had pushed a boulder to the top of a hill, only to watch it roll down again. The thought of trekking out to Elie on Friday was looking even less inviting than when he'd first read Vince's email, but trek he must.

Chapter 11

Sean had planned his journey carefully, but transport companies are no respecters of good planning. The Kirkcaldy train was late and the inevitable domino effect meant that he missed the bus he'd been intending to catch.

He bought a cup of coffee at a café near the bus station and soon regretted it. It tasted of something, of that he was sure, but coffee did not come into it. He drank about a third of it and found a drain into which to tip the remainder. He was not in any way a superstitious man, but the omens were looking very bad.

At last, a bus arrived and he wondered what sort of mood Vince would be in when he turned up late. Of course, he could, quite reasonably, ask Vince why he hadn't given him a lift in the first place, but this might not be the best time to mention it.

He got off the bus and hurried to the golf course as fast as his aching right knee would allow. It had rained overnight and the dampness seemed to have triggered the niggly arthritis he sometimes suffered in that joint.

At the course, he received his first piece of good news. Vince had not yet arrived and Sean went in search of a hot drink that might prove to be drinkable. He bought a rather expensive, but palatable, cup of tea and sat down to wait for the show to begin.

Vince walked in half an hour later. He gave no explanation for his lateness, but Sean wasn't remotely concerned about that. "Been here long?" Vince asked.

"A while," Sean replied truthfully, if non-committally.

Vince sat down and took a bottle of mineral water from his bag, along with some papers. He took a drink and said, "He shouldn't be too long. We can do some planning."

"Who is 'he', anyway?" asked Sean.

"Carl Engelhamer," said Vince. "From Texas. You won't miss him. He's about six-foot-five and big. Bit loud, but he's a good guy." He looked at his notes and said, "Marketing. We need some good marketing. What do you think about marketing?"

"Balls," muttered Sean.

"Pardon?" said Vince, looking up from his notes.

"Golf balls," said Sean. "Branded golf balls. V logo, bright colours, something like that."

"I like that," said Vince. "Write it down."

"How about luminous ones?" Sean suggested. "Bright pink or something?"

Vince shook his head vigorously. "I'm not having pink," he said. "Make it orange. Give the girls a ring – no, give Krystyna a ring and get her to look at balls." He gave a chuckle that sounded vaguely reminiscent of Sid James in a *Carry On* movie and said, "If you see what I mean."

Sean duly noted it all down and as he did so, became aware that there was not as much light as there had been when he'd started. He looked up to see a man of substantial proportions standing by the table.

"Mr Kingmyle," said the man who was evidently Carl Engelhamer.

Vince got to his feet and saw his hand vanish completely inside the vast mitt of the Texan. Although he introduced Sean, Engelhamer took little notice. He was more concerned with having his lunch before taking to the course.

Lunch was an experience that Vince and Engelhamer showed every sign of enjoying, though the same could not be said for Sean. He felt incidental to the event and found himself being referred to in the third person.

Nor was he helped by being a vegetarian. Not that the restaurant failed him in any way – in fact, they provided some good options – but his diet was received by the American with what might be described as disdain. In fact, Engelhamer declared that "real men eat meat". Sean, who was quite happy being an unreal man, merely shrugged his shoulders.

There were some consolations to be taken from the lunch. One was that Engelhamer was too busy shovelling food into his mouth to speak very much and a second was that the speed at which he did the shovelling meant that the meal was over relatively quickly.

After lunch, Vince got his client to sign some papers, which he then passed to Sean to take away. Not that Sean had any intention of traipsing all the way to Edinburgh on a Friday afternoon. He sat down in the bar and collected his various documents. While Vince and the American went to use the toilets before their game, he picked up his *Guardian*.

"See you on Monday, then," said Vince as he passed the table.

"Enjoy your game," Sean replied, fairly secure in the knowledge that this was unlikely.

Engelhamer ignored him and caught up with Vince. The man had a voice that matched his size, though it was a slightly high-pitched tone and carried with it the sense of a horse using a megaphone. "Commie paper, too," Sean heard him say. "You want to lose the pinko faggot," was the last line he caught before the pair left the building.

Sean got up from his seat and made an umbrella gesture at their backs. He watched them making their way towards the links. Vince, possibly seeking some inspiration from Gary Player, was dressed all in black. His paunch, and the fact the he leant forward slightly as he walked, gave him a rather waddling gait. He looked, Sean thought, somewhat like a large black duck that was attempting to do an impression of a penguin.

He limped over to the bar and the barman, who had been watching the performance, asked if he was okay.

"I've got a sore knee and a boss that's an idiot," Sean told him.

"Could be worse. At least it's Friday," the man replied.

Sean looked at the two handpumps on the bar and couldn't help but laugh when he saw the Bitter & Twisted pump clip of Harviestoun brewery.

"How apt," he said. He didn't normally drink during the day, but this was too inviting.

The barman pulled the pint. "I take it your boss is the one who's not the American," he said.

"Correct," Sean replied. "He's the one that looks like an overweight Atillio Lombardo."

Happily, the barman was of an age to remember the skilful Italian forward and at last, Sean found himself having an enjoyable conversation. He wasn't going to stay long, though, and as he neared the end of his pint, he rang Carol. "I've just met a real-life caricature," he told her, promising full details when he got home. There was a bus due in a few minutes and he intended to catch it. "That's enough of this lark for one week," he said.

Chapter 12

It was a sentiment with which Vince might well have concurred after a few holes in the company of Carl Engelhamer. Firstly, he'd continued to receive advice on how to run a business. Engelhamer, having reiterated the need to rid himself of the lefty weirdo, encouraged Vince to surround himself with 'hardbodies'. Vince wasn't entirely sure of what a hardbody was, but Engelhamer's additional teachings left him in little doubt.

The key, the American told him, was to employ women who were under thirty and unmarried. Trousers should be banned (Vince assumed that this only applied to women). On no account should children be involved. "They get pregnant, you fire 'em," Engelhamer said. "Thirtieth birthday, fire 'em, unless they're real lookers."

Vince was not a man given to self-doubt, but even he wondered if this would meet British employment law. Engelhamer punched Vince vigorously on his left biceps and said, "Always keep a note of their mistakes. Gross misconduct, every time. They got no comeback."

It was certainly interesting, thought Vince. He had to admit that the man had style. On the first tee, Engelhamer had produced a cigar that was only marginally shorter than Vince's putter, lit it and kept it wedged between his perfect teeth while playing and talking.

On that opening hole, Vince had noticed that the American was carrying a prodigious number of golf balls in his bag. When they played the first par-five hole on the course, the reason for this became evident.

Vince, while not the wizard of the links he imagined himself to be, was not a bad player. He had not played this course before, but could see the advantages of playing the hole conservatively. Getting to the green in two shots carried a high degree of risk; far better to hit the middle of the fairway and then lay up the second shot to leave a simple pitch for the third. That would provide a birdie opportunity. An eagle was out of the question, unless you got really lucky with the pitch.

Working along these lines, he played a safe, but highly satisfactory, drive to the centre of the fairway using a long iron. Engelhamer pulled out his driver. It was clear that he was intending to reach the green in two. Vince admired the bravado, but couldn't see it working.

The Texan launched his giant frame and the ball screamed off into the distance. While it travelled a long way forward, it also travelled a considerable way to the left. Thick rough and gorse bushes lay in wait. This, Vince thought, could be nasty for his new friend.

As Engelhamer's shot had been longer that Vince's, Vince played his second and did precisely as he had intended, leaving his ball some 100 yards short of the green, but with a pitching wedge, he trusted that he would leave himself with a shortish putt. Having played his shot, he turned left to help the American look for his ball.

He was surprised to find the man standing around with a broad grin on his face. "Fortune favours the brave, eh, Vince?" he said. He was standing in small patch of clear ground, on which his ball, or at least *a* ball, was sitting nicely. He proceeded to smack a three-iron shot that landed just short of the green and trickled slowly onto the putting surface.

As they walked to the green, Engelhamer gave Vince a further lecture on the advantages of being bold, whether that be in golf, business or life itself. There was no point, he said in pussyfooting around. You had to be forthright. Vince was in full agreement with the words, though he found it hard to dismiss the thought that he was being taken for a ride on the course.

It was a difficult afternoon for him. He was used to calling the shots, but he began to feel like a bit-part player. Fiercely competitive, he did not like to be beaten at anything, but he was uncomfortable at the idea of beating Engelhamer.

Not that Engelhamer had any intention of losing. As the round went on, the large bulge in his bag where he had put his wholesale supply of golf balls diminished noticeably. Vince felt as though he were playing against some unscrupulous villain from a *007* film. Indeed, the man had both the name and physical stature to make a very plausible villain.

Ultimately, the American triumphed by two shots, which Vince regarded as acceptable. They returned to the clubhouse where Engelhamer generously bought the drinks. Not that Vince was given any choice in the drink he was about to receive. Engelhamer had asked the barman for the oldest malt whisky that was available and to pour out two doubles.

Vince very rarely drank alcohol and certainly did not drink whisky. Recalling Engelhamer's views on Sean's vegetarianism, however, dissuaded him from taking a contrary view. Instead, he pretended to sip his drink until the giant Texan felt the need to go to the toilet. Vince checked that nobody was looking and tipped his (very expensive) malt into a nearby plant pot.

When Engelhamer returned, Vince assured him that he would keep in touch. "Good man," said Engelhamer, crushing Vince's hand for a second time that day while simultaneously giving him a thump on the back that made Vince wonder whether it was possible to dislocate a rib. The American lit another cigar as they left and Vince climbed into his car to drive home.

It had, he thought, been an educational day. He was not about to take up drinking malt whisky or smoking cigars and he was too old-fashioned to pull tricks like that on the golf course, but he had to admit, Engelhamer had a certain style. He was very taken with some of his ideas on business and began to think about women in skirts. Krystyna and Anne always wore trousers. Perhaps, he pondered, he should ban them. Was that legal? Probably not. Anyway, he mused, while Krystyna would doubtless look good in a skirt, the same couldn't be said for Anne. She was, quite frankly, short, fat and ugly. Perhaps he ought to fire her.

Chapter 13

Over the weekend, Vince gave a considerable amount of thought to what Carl Engelhamer had said on Friday. The American had pointed out that Vince's clientèle was almost exclusively male and that he, Vince, should recognise that and plan accordingly. It was, thought Vince, a valid observation and he considered ways of making his tours appeal to men.

As a result, he spent much of the weekend sitting in the spare room he had developed into an office, making copious notes and typing on his computer. His wife was rather taken aback by this activity, as Vince usually spent a goodly proportion of the weekend on a golf course. When she proffered a mild inquiry, he said that he was planning to take his business "to the next level".

If he was going to appeal to male golfers, he reasoned, then Engelhamer's view that a business needed some "eye candy" was a good one. Vince took a fresh sheet of paper – he only ever wrote on one side of a page – and wrote the names of his three employees at the top.

The first name was that of Sean Monaghan. Clearly, Sean did not fit into the eye-candy category. While Vince agreed with his American friend that Sean had some distinctly funny ideas, he was not gay. Carol was the evidence of that and while Vince could not abide that opinionated smart-Alec of a woman, she at least existed. Besides, Sean was very capable and had already proved his worth with the work he had done sorting out the spreadsheet nightmare.

He moved on to the second name on the page. He had written merely 'Krystyna' because he could not remember how to spell her infernally long surname. Now Krystyna fitted the bill as far as looks were concerned. She was slim, had a nice figure, a ready smile and enchanting eyes. She did, Vince thought ruefully, have a tendency to wear trousers. In fact, he could not recall seeing her wear anything but. Perhaps, he wondered, a Golf King uniform was required. He scribbled a note to that effect. Krystyna was also very capable, although Vince had noticed that she seemed to be getting on very well with Sean. He didn't mind that too much – after all, better that than have them fighting all the time – but he didn't want Krystyna turning into some art-loving bibliophile.

Finally, he came to the name 'Anne Kelly'. This was both the easiest and hardest to deal with. Anne could not, under any circumstances, be described as attractive. She was very short and she was overweight. She was also dim. She said little and did even less. There was, Vince decided, no good reason to keep her. Far better to find a – what did Engelhamer say? – a "hardbody" to take her place. Vince dutifully noted this down.

In the course of his deliberations, he also drew up a few adverts. He toyed with several ideas, but all were based around the theories of Carl Engelhamer. By Sunday evening, he had a whole raft of ideas about how to drive Golf King to the promised land.

On Monday, his plans were thrown into a degree of confusion. Anne had not appeared, as though she had experienced some form of premonition. She did, however, telephone the office and speak to Vince. Her son, who was five, was ill and she had taken him to hospital. She did not think that she would able to come to work this week.

Vince thought of Carl Engelhamer again once he had put the phone down. What had he said about women having children? This sort of thing bore out his comments, Vince felt. For the moment, he did nothing, but the thread by which Anne Kelly was hanging was growing thinner.

By Thursday, it had snapped. Anne had been in touch again. Her son would need to spend some time in hospital and she had no idea when she would be able to return. Vince knew that this was the moment. Not that he said anything on the phone – for one thing, Sean and Krystyna were there – but he sent Anne a text message to tell her not to come back.

"Anne won't be coming back," Vince announced on Friday morning. Sean and Krystyna had been aware of the illness that had befallen her child, but they were a little shocked at the news. Naturally, they assumed that Anne herself had made this decision and that the problem must be serious.

Krystyna, ensuring that she was out of range from Vince's hearing, approached Sean as he was making a cup of tea. "I thought we could get Anne a card and a leaving gift," she said.

"Good idea," Sean agreed. "I know it's a bit obvious, but how about some chocolates and flowers?"

"Obvious is not always wrong," Krystyna replied. She offered to get something at lunchtime and Sean gave her a £20 note.

Krystyna told Vince what she was planning to do, but she didn't know Anne's address or how to get the gifts to her. Vince said that he had Anne's address and that he would visit her home. He also said that he would take the few items that Anne had kept in the office.

Krystyna waited for Vince to put some money into the envelope that contained Sean's note and her own twenty pounds. "Would you like to contribute?" she asked hesitantly. Vince dug around in his jacket pocket and produced a pound coin. "Thank you so much," Krystyna said.

At lunchtime, she enlisted Sean's assistance and they bought a card, a bunch of flowers and a box of chocolates that at least looked as if they had been made with some care rather than churned out on a giant production line. Krystyna told Sean about the magnificent donation made by Vince.

"It's a step forward," Sean told her. "That's one pound more than he gave me for going to Elie the other day."

Vince, who was usually away early on a Friday afternoon, stayed late this time. He waited for Krystyna and Sean to leave, and was mildly irritated when the latter remained until nearly five o'clock. Eventually, Sean departed and Vince picked up the box into which he had placed Anne's belongings. He put the card, chocolates and flowers on top, switched off the lights and locked up.

He walked to his car and put the box on the back seat. Before he closed the door, he took out the card, which he, Sean and Krystyna had signed. He tore it in half and threw it into a litter bin. Then he got into his car and drove home.

Valerie was busy in the kitchen and Vince went to the spare room. He left the box there; he would arrange for a courier to deliver Anne's stuff. After all, he didn't want anyone to think he was stealing from the poor woman. He took the flowers and chocolates and went downstairs.

"Surprise," Vince said, presenting his wife with a bouquet of flowers.

"Goodness me," Valerie said, staring at the bright red bunch before her eyes.

"Second surprise," Vince added, whipping out the chocolates from behind his back.

"Oh, Vince, how thoughtful you are," his wife said.

"I know," Vince replied and sat down to enjoy his dinner.

Chapter 14

On Monday morning, Vince had so many ideas written down that he felt the need for a team meeting. Vince liked team meetings. They were, he felt, indicative of good management. He would set out his plans and the team could ask questions, as well as keeping everyone up to date with the work they were doing. This was how to manage, how to get the best out of people.

After a couple of hours pounding at his keyboard, Vince called his team together. They sat around a table and Vince revealed the fruits of his weekend's labour.

"We have," he announced, "a great opportunity. So far, we have brought golfers into Scotland. Now, we have the chance to send golfers from Scotland. Not just Scotland. Anywhere in Britain. I have important contacts in America. I know people in Spain and Portugal. Golf King Tours. What do you think of that?"

Sean and Krystyna knew better than to interrupt when Vince had a surge of missionary zeal. They also knew that it would be unwise to show anything less than enthusiasm. Both made sounds of complete approval.

Satisfied that he had their interest, Vince continued. "This is a fantastic opportunity to put Golf King on the map. This is our big chance. When we get this up and running, it could be monumentous. It's the big one and we need to grab the bullet by the horns."

Sean glanced across at Krystyna. She was looking straight ahead and it seemed that her eyes had glazed over. Sean empathised. He felt that his brain had glazed over.

Vince was oblivious. The enormity of his mission was carrying him forward and his train of thought, loaded with its cargo of new enterprise, steamed on down the track. "We need to get the word out there. There's one thing that is paramount – advertising, advertising, advertising. We need publicity, we need people to know what we're doing, see how good we are."

He sat back and looked at his two remaining staff. Sean gave it a few seconds to see if another blast was forthcoming and asked, "Does this mean we need extra staff?"

Vince nodded. "We need somebody soon. Just one to start with, then we'll see how it grows. I want someone who can go out and meet people. A kind of sales rep. She's got to be good, though. I'm going to make sure we get the right person."

"She?" said Krystyna.

Vince looked at her, but made no reply.

"You said 'she'," Krystyna continued.

"Yes," Vince said. He offered no further explanation and Krystyna could see there was no future in pursuing the point.

Vince turned over his notes and said, "Ah, yes, here's another idea that I had. Branded golf balls." Failing to notice the exchange of glances between Sean and Krystyna, he went on, "I want to get some golf balls made with the Golf King logo. I want them to stand out. Bright orange, bright yellow, something that grabs the attention."

Sean told Vince that he had already made some enquiries with manufacturers. This seemingly innocuous remark sent Vince's wagons careering off the rails.

"There's no point in me carrying on, is there?" Vince said, sarcastically. "No point in me being the manager if Sean is going to make all the decisions. Who's running this team?"

Sean allowed a gentle smile to pass across his face as he was referred to in the third person. "It's not a question of making decisions," he said placidly, "it's simply getting the information that allows us to make decisions. All I did was see if they could make what we want and get some prices."

Vince glared at him. "Oh, so he just decides who he's going to have a meeting with, without informing his manager."

Sean continued to regard his boss with wry amusement and, unable to resist continuing the third person role, said, "Isn't he allowed to talk to relevant people about work matters, then?"

"You're undermining me," Vince shouted. "I'm the manager, I'm in charge and you should tell me what you're doing. You shouldn't be making decisions universally."

"Unilaterally," Sean said quietly, "and I'm not. I'm consulting people."

Vince continued to glare. "Yes, everyone except me, the one person who counts," he said, throwing his pen at the table in front of him, but missing. Sean picked it up. "You dropped this," he said. Vince snatched it from his hand and clipped it into his shirt pocket.

The meeting ended and Vince marched back to his desk, put on his jacket and went out to get his lunchtime cup of soup. Krystyna looked at Sean with some anxiety.

"Are you okay?" she asked.

"Me?" said Sean, instantly realising that this was a stupid thing to say, he being the only other person in the office. "Fine," he said. "He likes to let off steam every now and then."

"But you were only doing what he asked you to do in this first place," said Krystyna.

"I know," Sean said, "but there's no point in bringing logic into it."

Krystyna smiled. She suspected that Sean had witnessed several eruptions from Mount Vince over the years. "I need to go out," she said. "Come on, let me buy you a cup of coffee."

Sean was happy to accept. He usually sat and read his paper at lunchtime, but some fresh air and a cup of coffee sounded like a great idea. As they walked down the road, Vince was coming back with his soup. He ignored the pair of them.

"Could be a long afternoon," Krystyna said.

Sean shook his head. "He'll be all right soon, once he's had his soup."

"I wonder what's in it," Krystyna said.

"Magic mushrooms," said Sean.

Chapter 15

With an extra member of staff required, Vince wrote an advertisement. Fortunately, he passed it to Krystyna to place it with the Edinburgh Evening News and she ensured that the copious errors were corrected before she sent it off. She removed commas from places they shouldn't have been, inserted commas into places they should have been, deleted apostrophes from plural words and amended various spelling mistakes.

Sean, who was looking at the same screen, said, "You'd think that with two people who have studied literature in the office, he might trust us to write letters by ourselves."

Krystyna sighed. "Do you think he knows that there is a spellchecker on Word?"

"He probably thinks that it's wrong and he's right," Sean said.

Vince was, for the moment, out somewhere, but with the recruitment process started, this would change. He had told Sean to create a mailbox for the sole purpose of receiving applications. Once Sean had done this, Vince immediately restricted access to himself.

Krystyna had suggested placing an advert in the nearby Job Centre.

Vince quickly vetoed that idea. "No chance," he said. "All we'll get is a load of workshy neds."

"If they are workshy, why would they apply for a job?" Krystyna asked with an alarming degree of logic.

"You haven't lived in this country long enough to understand," Vince said, putting an end to the incipient discussion.

Sean, who was busying himself trying to make the Golf King website look at least half decent, kept out of the debate. He knew from long experience that trying to make a point using reason was like trying to start a fire with an ice lolly when Vince had a fixed idea in his mind. He was far from convinced that there would be many applicants of any description, let alone the stream of nubile females that Vince seemed to be expecting.

Vince, who had been irritated that he was unable to be more specific about his requirements in the advert's text, sat and waited, keeping an eye on the new mailbox. Little happened for the first couple of days, but then came an avalanche, at least in relative terms.

"Four applications," Vince told his colleagues. "Now we're tearing up the fast lane."

More like the bus lane, thought Sean, though wisely, he chose not to share that thought.

Vince's initial enthusiasm was dampened when he discovered that three of them were from men. The fourth was from a woman in her forties. This was not what he was looking for. He did no more than look at the names and ages before consigning them to the recycle bin.

Even so, the applications kept coming, though most of them served merely to irritate Vince even more. Sean and Krystyna always knew when he was looking at them, as a constant stream of heavy sighs emanated from the direction of his desk.

"Half of them can't even spell properly," Vince said with some distaste.

Neither of his staff passed any comment and Sean avoided eye contact with Krystyna. Instead, he sent her an email that read: *Lecture from Professor Kingmyle on speling and gramer.*

Seconds later, Krystyna made a strange noise that she hurriedly converted into a sneeze. She hit the reply button on the email and wrote back: *Applicant's for job's are not litterate.*

Vince, oblivious to the electronic messages buzzing all around him, despatched yet more job applications into the void. This exercise was not proving as simple as he'd hoped. The majority had been from men and these he had binned as soon as he had seen their names. He had not even bothered to open the attachments. Those from women were given a little more attention.

These did not always show an age, so he had been forced into looking at the CV to get an idea of it from their past experience.

It seemed to take an age, but he finally collected enough twenty-something women to give him some hope, declaring the recent arrivals to be "more better". He had a list of three and he gave Krystyna instructions to invite them to interviews. It did not escape her attention that his prospective employees were all female and young.

"What is this, a beauty contest?" she asked Sean, after Vince had gone on the soup run.

Sean had a fair idea. "It's that American clown he played golf with the other week," he explained. "He'll probably fill the place with 'eye candy'," he added, trying with no great success, to impersonate a Texan accent. "Probably boot us out, as well."

"Us?" said Krystyna. "You mean that I am not eye candy?" She was smiling.

"You're not blonde," Sean told her. "That could be significant."

"Oh God," Krystyna said, "what next? Bikinis at golf courses? That's it – he is trying to make golf like motor racing. What do they call those girls with umbrellas?"

"Umbrella girls," Sean said.

Krystyna narrowed her eyes. "Very funny."

"But they are," Sean said. "That's what they call them."

"Oh," said Krystyna. "Anyway, that is it. And boxing – the girl who goes in the ring with the board to show the next round. He will have a girl in a bikini showing the number of the hole."

They heard the front door open and Sean said hurriedly and in a whisper, "For God's sake don't suggest any of that. He'd do it."

Chapter 16

So it was that Krystyna was surprised when Vince asked her to invite to interview a young man from Leeds. Glancing at his CV, she saw that he had studied at Edinburgh University and was presently employed by an insurance company. Krystyna's English was colloquial enough to be aware of the phrase 'out of the frying pan and into the fire', but she did her duty. For some reason, Vince had requested that this be the first interview.

"Why do you think he has invited a man?" Krystyna asked Sean.

Sean shrugged his shoulders. "Who knows?" he said. Even after several years of Vince's management, he was never confident about apportioning reasons to any decisions made by Vince.

"Another foreigner, too," Krystyna giggled.

"Good point," Sean acknowledged. "Anybody would think he's been doing diversity training."

A week later, Vince had made one of his many short disappearances from the office when the buzzer sounded from the front door. Krystyna, who was nearest, jumped up and went to see who it was. Sean continued to stare balefully at the web page he was trying, without a great deal of success, to make look professional. He heard the brief conversation, however.

"Hi, I'm Mick Jackson. I'm due to have an interview at eleven."

"Oh, yes, come in. Mr Kingmyle is not here at the moment, but he will not be long. Please, come in and wait."

Sean looked up to see a fair-haired young man of about twenty-three. Krystyna introduced them to each other and asked Mick if he'd like a tea or coffee.

"Coffee, please," Mick said and Sean gestured to him to sit

down. They chatted amiably and Sean discovered that Mick, not surprisingly, was a Leeds United supporter.

"Dear me," Sean said, "you have my sympathy."

"I know," said Mick with a gloomy smile. "One crisis to the next. We're a shambles."

The next few minutes of Mick's life may well have persuaded him that his beloved club were not, after all, in such a bad state. It was possible that he may have preferred to reserve the word 'shambles' for something else. Either way, he underwent an experience he was unlikely to forget, however hard he might wish otherwise.

When Vince returned, he took Mick through to a small room at the back of the office. They sat down and Vince, though he had no intention of offering the job to the young Yorkshireman, waxed lyrical about Golf King and its future. After ten minutes, Mick was left in no doubt that this was a company on the verge of greatness.

Satisfied that Vince had completed his eulogy, Mick asked, "So what would my role be?"

Vince leant back in his chair for a moment, picked up his pen and then leaned forward to address his interviewee. "Nothing is black or white at the moment," he said. "Marketing is the big thing at the moment. We want to compete with the bigger players. They don't care about us and we want to be starting something." He smiled knowingly and continued, "Your job – if you get the job, of course – can be anything you want it to be. Nothing dangerous, it goes without saying. We are not here to heal the world. We intend to beat the world, you understand? Beat it!"

Mick began to wonder if the man sitting across the desk from him was entirely sane. He'd been to plenty of interviews before, but not one like this. For one thing, Vince did not seem to have the slightest interest in anything he had done, what his skills were or any of those other things that people asked you when you were after a job. The man simply kept babbling.

Vince moved onto golf. "Do you play?" he asked.

Mick, sensing that a negative response might not be judicious, said, "A bit. I don't get much time to, though."

Vince was undeterred and began to run through a catalogue of the iconic courses he had played. The most difficult, he declared, had been Carnoustie, where the wind had been driving in from the North Sea and he had been up against an experienced local in a match-play tournament.

"You could hardly walk into the wind," Vince said. "It was blowing in rain as well. This guy was a good player and he knew the course like the back of his hand. I was three down at the turn and got one back, but then he won the next hole and I won one again. I was two down with three to play. I was bunkered on the sixteenth, but chipped out stone dead and won the hole. Only one down. Seventeenth, I hit a three iron into the wind, but drilled it low and ended up eight feet from the flag. Holed the putt – all square with one to play. We both hit perfect drives on the last and he played first. Good iron shot, right to the heart of the green. My shot was perfect, but the wind caught it and threw it left, just off the green. Pitch or putt? I was off the putting surface. I was in a jam. I thought 'This is it'. I putted and started it six feet to the left of the hole. I read the break perfectly. It dropped and he missed his long putt and I won by one stroke. Thriller!"

Mick, who had commendably stayed awake, had no idea what to say. It mattered little, as Vince gave his charge an edited highlights package of his sporting career and left the Yorkshireman wondering where the nearest pub was and whether it was open yet.

The interview, if it could be so termed, went on for over an hour until Vince decided that he had covered all of the important points. They emerged back into the main office and as they neared the door, Vince said, "Well, thank you for coming in. We'll let you know."

Mick, who had borne everything with superhuman stoicism, straightened his back and looked Vince in the eye. "Don't bother yourself," he said. "I wouldn't work for a jerk like you for a hundred grand a week." He spun sharply on his heel and walked out with a surprisingly jaunty air.

Vince, who had been too dumbstruck to respond, muttered, "Rude idiot. Why do I waste my time with these people?"

Sean, who had watched the scene with wry amusement, said, "Bad, was he?"

Vince opened his mouth to reply and then stopped and glared at Sean. "Idiot," he hissed, not making it clear whether he meant Sean or Mick. He snatched up his jacket and walked out of the office. Soup was the only answer.

Chapter 17

A quiet Friday morning at the office of Golf King Ltd was interrupted by the arrival of Carol Whelan shortly after half past ten. She had come to leave a bag with Sean while she went to visit an art gallery.

Carol's cheerful "Good morning" was reciprocated by Krystyna. Vince made a noise that could have been construed as a greeting, but sounded more like a meerkat with a cough. Vince did not like Carol and the feeling was mutual. After the first meeting between the pair, Sean had noted, not without some approval, that Carol had taken an instant dislike to Vince. Carol's reply had been, "Well, it saves time, doesn't it?"

Nevertheless, Carol was prepared to indulge her foe and said, "I hear that business is booming."

Vince, whose ego was never averse to a massage, could not hide his enthusiasm. "We are. We're cooking the gas," he said.

"Better use the right gas, then," Carol said. "Many gases are highly combustible."

"Not just gases," muttered Sean, who received an approving wink from his partner.

Krystyna asked Carol how she was getting on with her thesis. Carol's reply had barely left the starting platform when Vince interceded.

Staring fixedly at his computer monitor, he said, "Krystyna, I want you to phone somebody. Now."

Carol gave Krystyna a pat on the arm and said, "Don't panic, Corporal." She moved away from the desks and said, "Okay, I'm off. I'll be back when the Prince of Darkness has done his work."

Vince continued to gaze at a point on his monitor, but a discernible twitch came across his face.

"The exhibition I'm going to," lied Carol to the bemused Krystyna, "is a celebration of early Gothic painting. Dark and scary. Creepy castles and dungeons, vampires, you name it." She poked her tongue out in the direction of Vince, who was steadfast in his determination not to catch her laser-beam grey eyes. She winked at Sean again, turned and departed, quietly singing "House of Fun" as she left.

Vince said little during the remainder of the morning. There was something about that woman that nettled him. What, he thought, gave her the right to waltz into his office as if she owned the place? He'd have thrown her out if it had not been for Sean. Perhaps he ought to have a word with Sean about it.

By the time he had his lunch spread out on his desk, he was feeling better. He had bought his soup and newspapers and there was a story in *The Sun* that had the effect of making him angry, yet happy at the same time. A painting by one of the Dutch Masters had sold in London for 12 million pounds. This, to Vince's mind, was ridiculous, but it gave him the opportunity to hit back at art and art lovers, against whom he held a permanent grudge, but especially so after the experiences of the morning.

With withering contempt, he read aloud from his paper. Satisfied that he had the attention of his staff, he said, "What idiot would pay that for a painting. I wouldn't pay 12p for that rubbish. It's not even any good." He looked round to see if there were any challengers. His eyes fixed on Sean.

Sean didn't really feel like getting into an argument he knew was unwinnable. Even so, there was a principle at stake and he knew that this onslaught was, essentially, an attack on Carol. He made a game effort.

"We're talking about something that's five centuries old," he said. "The cost of that would just about cover Gareth Bale's right arm," he added, putting it into a currency that Vince might comprehend. "How long does a footballer last? Fifteen years at most. Great art lasts for ever."

Vince, naturally enough, was not having it. "Millions of people watch football," he said. "Who looks at pictures? A few posers with too much money. Normal people don't bother themselves with that sort of rubbish."

"I look at pictures," Sean replied equably. "I might be a poser and it's very possible that I'm not normal, but I definitely haven't got any money." He went on, "I've got a photo at home. It's taken from inside The Hermitage in Saint Petersburg. People queuing to get in. Queues going back miles. And they look like pretty ordinary people."

Vince pulled a face. "More fool them," he said.

"Okay, it's expensive," Sean conceded, "but things have cost more. A couple of years back, a Botticelli—"

Vince interrupted him. "Well, at least I agree with you on that one. Manchester City should never have paid that much for him."

Sean opened his mouth, then closed it again. He decided to leave things where they lay. He knew a lost cause when he saw one.

Chapter 18

Monday mornings at the offices of Golf King held two certainties. One was that Vince would arrive in the office after ten o'clock. The other was that he would have at least one new idea that he would unveil as if it were the sculpture of a famous person. This particular Monday was no exception.

"I need a new website," he told Sean.

"In place of the Golf King one or in addition to it?" Sean asked.

"Golf King is business," Vince said. "I need a personal website. Can you set one up?"

"If you give me the details of exactly what you want, I'll see what I can do," Sean said.

"We can have a meeting to discuss the details," Vince said airily. "I thought vk.com would be a good name, if we can start there."

"No go with that one," Sean told him.

Vince frowned. "What do you mean, 'no go'?" he asked.

"You'd have to go to war with Russia," Sean said. He took a moment to enjoy the puzzlement on Vince's face and went on, "It's a whacking great social-media site, vk.com. Like the Russian equivalent of Facebook. Even Bill Gates would be struggling to buy that name off them."

"You're joking," said Vince, looking at Krystyna for confirmation that Sean was merely playing mind games.

"He's right," she said. "It's very big. Millions of users."

"Type vk.com into your search engine and it'll come up straight away," Sean added.

Vince sat down, evidently devastated by the news. He added a couple of notes to the sheet of paper that contained his plans and said, "Never mind, we'll have a meeting this afternoon. We need to do it today, so if we start after lunch, we can get the basics down by five o'clock. Don't forget, I've got a busy week."

It was indeed a busy week. Vince had arranged for interviewees to come in on Tuesday, Wednesday and Thursday. By the time the third one had been ushered into the interview room at the back of the office, certain things had become clear.

"Another one," Krystyna said to Sean after Vince had closed the door.

Sean nodded. "All early twenties and all blonde." He looked at Krystyna and said, "Ever thought of dying your hair?"

Krystyna fingered a strand of her dark hair. "Very funny," she said.

Almost three hours later, there was still no sign of life emerging from the interview room. Sean walked round to Krystyna's desk and asked, "Do you think we should call the police?"

"Or an ambulance? Or both?" Krystyna suggested.

Fifteen minutes later, Vince reappeared, beaming broadly and still in deep conversation with his would-be employee. The pair passed Sean and Krystyna on the way, but the existence of neither was acknowledged. Vince led his charge to the front door and it was another fifteen minutes before he returned to his desk. He had the expression of a very large cat that had pilfered a chicken coop.

"I think we have a result," he announced. "No contest, in fact."

Krystyna waited for a few seconds to see if more wisdom was about to be dispensed. It wasn't, and she asked, "So, you will need me to write a letter?"

Vince appeared to be lost in a reverie somewhere, but came to and replied, "No, there's no need. I will email Laura myself and sort out the details of when she starts. She will definitely take the job. Perfect result, we will be ideal for her and she will be ideal for us. Outstanding candidate by miles."

Krystyna shrugged slightly and Sean carried on with his

website. It was clear to both of them that Vince had been overwhelmed by whatever talents and charms that Laura possessed, as was evidenced by the remaining half hour or so that Vince spent in the office. He embarked on a monologue that featured, with some regularity, the phrases "Laura says", "Laura wants to" and "Laura will be". Finally he put on his jacket, picked up his briefcase and left his remaining staff to wonder what they were letting themselves in for.

Not that either of them were planning to hang around for long. Krystyna was putting her jacket on while Sean was speaking to Carol on the phone. She started slightly when Sean began to sing "Tell Laura I Love Her" into the receiver, then started to giggle. She crushed a piece of paper and threw it at Sean. With impressive accuracy, it bounced off his temple and landed on the floor beside him.

Sean, unperturbed, continued his conversation. "I've got a bad feeling about this," he told Carol, and he was not referring to the small missile that had hit him. He waved to the departing Krystyna and went on, "He gets this fixation with certain women. It's happened before."

"He's got a fixation with me," Carol said. "He hates my guts."

"I think it's more your brain that he hates," Sean said. "I wish you'd turned up this afternoon, actually. It was like he'd been taking laughing gas. You'd have deflated him."

"I'll lend you my rifle then. Just a small bore," Carol said ambiguously. It was a sentiment Sean fully understood.

Chapter 19

After such an exhausting week, Vince decided that Friday should be taken at a more leisurely pace. He arrived at the office at quarter to eleven, perused a few emails and spent an hour on the phone talking about the defensive frailties of the Heart of Midlothian defence. After describing in some detail how he, as someone who had played at the highest level, would address those frailties, he had lunch, replied to a couple of the more interesting emails and departed.

"Another long day, I see," Sean observed after Vince had taken his leave.

"At least he is in his happy mode," Krystyna observed. "He is very up and down; some days he is very angry, some days he is very happy, some days he does not speak."

"He's always been like that," Sean told her. "Ever since I can remember. He's up and down like a hippo on a trampoline."

While Krystyna conjured with that appalling image, Sean picked up his phone to see what Carol was doing, as he knew she was in Edinburgh.

"I'm at Tollcross," she told him. "I've just been to the organic shop, like the liberal trendy I am."

That gave Sean an idea. "Have you got anything else you need to do?" he asked.

"Well, I need to put on my balaclava and get out my AK-47 and rob the bank," she said.

This, Sean surmised correctly, meant 'no'. He said, "The King has left the building, so I think it's only fair if the lackeys follow suit."

"Another long day?" said Carol. "How about Cloisters Bar? I can't see any danger of running into VK there."

"No chance," Sean affirmed. "He'll be heading for the golf course."

"Get Krystyna to come along, if she fancies it," Carol said. "I wouldn't like to think of the poor girl sitting in the office on her own until five."

Krystyna, while liking the idea in principle, was slightly worried by the idea of disappearing this early in the day.

"Vince did," Sean pointed out.

"Yes, but it is his business," Krystyna reasoned. "He can do what he likes."

"True," Sean agreed, "but he's going to play golf. That means there's no chance he'll come back here. There's also no chance that he will bother to phone, either."

"What about customers?" Krystyna asked.

"They can leave a message on the answerphone. Nothing can be that urgent. It's not like this is a casualty department. What do we do? We take money from people with too much time and too much money who want to play golf. Whoopee. Plus, it's Friday afternoon, so 95% of our potential customers will be out on the golf course, just like The Great Leader."

Krystyna smiled. She knew that Sean was right and as she pointed out, both she and Sean would be in the office long before Vince on Monday morning, by which time they would have dealt with any messages. Having convinced herself that this was entirely sensible, she shut down her computer and headed for the pub.

Vince, meanwhile, was continuing to dispense wisdom to Stuart Webster, with whom he had been talking during his morning phone call. He and Stuart were enjoying a round at one of the many clubs that Vince had joined. Stuart had not played this course before and was impressed.

So impressed, in fact, that he suggested to Vince that they make an evening of things. Vince was not one of life's natural party animals, but he was still on a high after a very successful week and from the excellent form he had been displaying on the course, especially with his putter. Dutiful husband that he was, he phoned Valerie and explained that he had received an unexpected invitation from a friend and would not be home until late in the evening.

It is probably reasonable to assume that Vince was not completely prepared for what Stuart had in store for him. They had remained in the clubhouse for a while, where Vince had his usual choice of soft drink while he enthused to his friend about the success of his recruitment campaign. Stuart may have had little in common with either Sean or Krystyna, but like them he could see that Laura had made quite an impression on Vince.

They moved on and Vince took Stuart to his favourite West End club. This was another location new to Stuart and he felt that he owed Vince something stronger than slimline tonic water.

"Have a proper drink," he said. "Come, on we're having a night on the town."

Vince was concerned about his car.

"Leave it where it is," Stuart told him. "It's in the New Town. What's going to happen to it there?"

Vince acceded and accepted a half pint of lager. He certainly wasn't going to try any of that weird real-ale stuff that Sean liked drinking.

The party was in full swing. After three halves, Vince was ready to be led further into the mysteries of the night and found himself alongside Stuart in the back of a taxi heading down Leith Walk. Vince glanced to his right at the side streets that ran through to Easter Road and gave an involuntary shudder. This was Hibernian territory.

After a couple more at a bar that was, to Vince, remarkably salubrious, they moved on again. The bar that Stuart had chosen had two well-built, black-clad gentlemen on the door. To Vince's surprise, they appeared to be familiar with his friend, who chatted amiably with them for a minute before guiding Vince inside.

The entertainment was already underway. Vince noted, with a slightly bleary eye, that the establishment was staffed, largely, by young ladies wearing a very limited amount of clothing. Stuart, who appeared to know quite a number of people, bought drinks and told Vince, with a knowing nod and nudge, that his 'side dish' would arrive soon.

This may have been unfamiliar territory for Vince, but he was feeling pleasantly befuddled and was game for anything. A girl with blonde hair and impressive figure approached the table and slid easily onto Stuart's lap.

"Back again?" she said with a grin. "You just can't keep away, can you?"

"Just bringing you some extra custom, Sophie," Stuart said, patting her left thigh. Sophie grinned at Vince and blew an air kiss in his direction. "You go and give my friend Vince some of your special attention. I'll wait my turn."

"Okay," Sophie said. She whispered in Stuart's ear, "I'll get you one of the new girls. How about Vicky? She's hot. We call her 'Vicky the Vixen'."

Stuart chuckled and said, "Sounds good to me. Bring her on."

Sophie draped herself over Vince and put her arms around his neck. Vince's eyes, which under normal circumstances had a frog-like protuberance, bulged even more as Sophie's breasts threatened to do them some untold damage. Sophie was aware that Vince's eyes were not the only part of his anatomy that was bulging.

Stuart looked on with detached amusement and took a sip of the whisky he'd ordered. He was in no hurry. He been here plenty of times. There was, naturally enough, quite a high turnover of staff and it was quite normal for there to be one or two new girls. He'd soon enough see what this one was like, but for now he entertained himself by watching Vince as Sophie gyrated on his lap.

Vince was enjoying the attention. Sophie was certainly a

good-looking girl, he thought, and she was undoubtedly close enough for him to appreciate her finer points. He glanced across at Stuart, whose girl had not yet arrived. Stuart gave him a thumbs up.

With Sophie's voluptuous body blocking much of his peripheral vision, Vince saw little of the girl who had approached Stuart. Vince was aware of her presence, but little more. He could see, as the girl settled on Stuart's lap, that she was slender and evidently very young.

Suddenly, Sophie leant back, giving Vince a larger field of vision. He looked across at Stuart and then to the girl. Vince made a strange noise that made Sophie, Stuart and 'The Vixen' look at him. Vince found himself staring into the terrified eyes of his daughter Victoria.

Chapter 20

A Saturday-morning hangover is not entirely unknown for those enjoying an evening out in Edinburgh and so it was that the entire workforce of Golf King Ltd, along with Carol Whelan, were feeling a little less than sprightly after their adventures.

Krystyna, introduced to the pleasures of cask-conditioned ale by Sean and Carol, had woken early and taken remedial action. She drank a litre of water, took two paracetamol and returned to bed, where she promptly fell asleep again. When she awoke, two hours later, things did not seem so bad.

Sean and Carol had been up early as well. They had eaten breakfast and drunk several glasses of fruit juice and cups of tea. Sean retired to bed to read a book while Carol lay in the bath and read the newspaper. When she emerged and looked in the bedroom, she found that Sean had fallen asleep with the book lying on his throat. She gently removed it and put it on the bedside cabinet. "Good idea," she whispered and lay down on the bed. She, too, fell asleep and the pair of them felt a great deal better by midday.

At least the problems faced by Krystyna, Sean and Carol were purely of a physical nature. The same could not be said for the Managing Director of Golf King Ltd.

Vince woke up on the sofa with a large erection and an even larger hangover. In a moment of unusual sagacity, he ignored the former and concentrated on the latter. Not that he could really ignore it. He sat up and found a bottle of water lying at his feet. He drank some of it and tried to remember what had happened.

He had no difficulty recalling the ghastly moment when his eyes had met those of his daughter. He remembered her scream and there had been a lot of shouting, much of it by himself. He knew that one of the gorillas dressed in dinner suits had manhandled him and that he had ended up outside on the pavement. Then there had been the shouting match with Stuart and he vaguely remembered calling his friend – probably ex-friend by now – a pervert and several other choice names.

Of course, Stuart could hardly know that Vince's daughter would be part of the entertainment. Even Vince realised that, but as far as he could see, none of this would have happened had it not been for Stuart Webster and his sordid hobbies. Vince finished the water and threw the empty bottle onto the carpet.

He had become aware of an unpleasant and slightly sweet smell pervading the living room and he looked around to see if he could identify the source. Eventually, his eyes alighted on his shoes, which gave the appearance of having been worn in a muddy field. He picked them up and sniffed cautiously. He recoiled; there was the unmistakable smell of vomit.

Just as he put the soiled footwear down, his wife appeared. She looked at him for a moment and said, "Comfortable night?"

Vince did not completely miss the note of sarcasm in her tone. He bought himself a little thinking time by standing up and straightening the cushions. "It seemed best to sleep here," he said. "I didn't want to disturb you."

To his surprise, Valerie laughed scornfully. "You didn't want to disturb me," she repeated. "So coming in rolling drunk after midnight, babbling like a lunatic at the top of your voice and throwing up on the kitchen floor is not disturbing me?"

"Oh," said Vince.

Valerie glared at him. "So you don't remember any of that?" she said.

Vince shuffled uncomfortably. He was tempted to ask just what he had been babbling, but decided that it was, on the whole, not the best question. He struggled to think of anything that might have resembled even a half-decent question. He gave up on the idea of questions and said, "Somebody spiked my drink. You know I never drink."

Valerie wasn't buying it. "And somebody spiked your next

drink, and the one after that and the one after that, did they?" she said.

Vince decided that making a peace offering was the way forward. "I'll clean up the kitchen," he said. Even this got him nowhere.

"I did it last night," Valerie told him. "I don't want my kitchen smelling like some squalid pub."

Vince sat down again. He tried to think of something sensible to say, but his head was hurting too much to perform any kind of computation. One thing he was able to work out was that anything resembling the truth was inadvisable. Finally, he asked, "Where's Victoria?"

"Luckily for her, she's staying with a friend," Valerie said.

"What friend?" asked Vince suspiciously.

"Diane, if you must know," Valerie answered.

"Who's Diane?" Vince asked.

"They went to school together," said Valerie. "Why, what do you want her for?"

Vince had an answer for that, but wisely decided not to use it. "Just wondered," he said meekly.

Valerie said no more. She went into the hall and picked up her jacket and handbag. "I'm going out," she said. "I'm not going to be back until late, by which time you will have cleaned yourself and your shoes up. If you can face eating, you know where the kitchen is."

Vince had no reply to give. He was just about to lie down again when his wife returned.

"Where's the car?" she demanded.

"In Edinburgh," Vince told her. "I'm not stupid enough to drive while—"

Valerie's raised eyebrow was enough to stop him. She put her hand out. "Keys," she said.

Vince got up again and found, to his relief, that the car keys were in his jacket pocket. He handed them over. He told Valerie where he had left the car and this time, she left. Vince crumpled to the sofa and attempted to work out a strategy. This was going to take all of his managerial genius, but for now, the only sensible option appeared to be to go back to sleep.

Chapter 21

Krystyna's fears that the telephones would be inundated on Friday afternoon were, as Sean had suspected, unfounded. There were two calls, one of which was an automated message offering to reduce energy bills. She rang the other caller and left a message on his answerphone to say that she had called back.

Sean arrived at ten to nine and they worked on the basis that it would be a good hour before Vince arrived. The hour passed and then another.

"Wonder where Phil is today," Sean mused.

"Phil?" asked Krystyna.

"Short for Philistine," Sean explained. "Another one of Carol's little jokes."

"He'll probably come in for his lunch," Krystyna said, smiling at the thought of Carol's scathing assessments.

Another half an hour passed and the phone rang. Krystyna picked it up and after a brief and one-sided conversation, relayed the news.

"Vince is not coming in," she said. "Working from home, he says."

"Probably catching up with football," Sean guessed.

This time, Sean's suspicions were wrong. Vince, having spent the weekend thinking that if he'd wanted to go to Coventry, he would have bought a train ticket, at last found somebody who would speak to him in the shape of his daughter. It was not, however, a conversation he enjoyed.

"I trust that you've quit that disgusting bar," Vince said.

"Yes," mumbled Victoria, playing the role of sullen teenager with a natural ease.

Vince waited for more, but the ball was on his side of the net. He decided to adopt the role of disappointed father.

"I feel let down," he said. "I expected better of you."

There was no reply, though he suspected that the feeling might be mutual.

"Why?" he asked. "What possessed you to do it?"

Victoria, who had been taking a close interest in her fingernails, looked up. She shrugged. Then she decided that a counterattack was necessary.

"Look, Dad, I went to work behind the bar, right? I didn't go there to be a dancer. They offered me more money if I'd do that. I just thought, why not?"

"I can't believe his," Vince said.

"Well, it's true. And nothing happens, okay? Nothing at all. It's just dirty old men getting cheap thrills, nothing else."

Vince, who had just about enough self-awareness to realise that taking the moral high ground was not really one of the available options, could find no response for a few seconds.

"It stops right here," he said eventually.

"It already has," Victoria told him. "It stopped about ten seconds after they threw you out."

Vince coloured. "I was not thrown out," he said huffily. "I left once I had discovered what I went there to find out. I'd heard what was going on and decided to investigate."

If Vince assumed that Victoria was going to be cowed into a grovelling apology so that she could be welcomed back as the prodigal daughter, he was very wrong. There was determination in her eyes. "Dad, please. I've seen the video tapes and there are all sorts of photos as well."

Vince stared at her. "What photos? What tapes?" he demanded.

"The place has CCTV," Victoria explained calmly. "And there's a resident photographer. There's always loads of photos."

Vince's stare turned to a glare. "And who's got all of these things?" he asked.

Victoria shrugged again. "Lots of people," she said.

Vince stood up. Had the Kingmyle family possessed a cat, the odds were that the unfortunate animal would have been on the end of a shoeing at that moment. In the absence of a feline, Vince jabbed his foot at his golf bag. He stared out of the living-room window for a few seconds, then spun round. "Right," he said. "None of this goes further. None of this gets to your mother. I will not say anything and you will not say anything. Deal?"

"Fair enough," Victoria said with a nonchalance that Vince found galling.

"Right," said Vince again. "I'm going to play golf. And you – you find yourself a more respectable occupation, please. We'll have no more of this nonsense."

He swung his golf bag onto his shoulder and left with as much dignity as he could manage. Victoria remained sitting at the dinner table and watched him load the clubs into his car and drive off. She leaned back in her chair and exhaled. As far as she knew, there was no CCTV at the pub and she certainly was not aware of a house photographer. There was, though, absolutely no need for her father to know any of this.

Chapter 22

The week continued to provide frustrations for Vince. An errant daughter was one thing, but a business that was not running as smoothly as desired was another. Perhaps, he mused as he drove to the office on Tuesday morning, it was time for an overhaul.

He spent much of the morning compiling lists. Vince liked lists. They provided a sense of order and meaning. You could learn a lot from a list and for the first, he wrote 'Attributes' at the top of the page, with two columns headed 'Good' and 'Bad' underneath. He devised a system of marks for each attribute and applied each property to Sean and Krystyna, adding and subtracting as necessary. He counted the totals and added a note at the bottom. It read, 'Need to up their game'.

It was, of course, only fair that he, as manager, should be assessed accordingly. He assigned marks to his own skills and found only positives. He kept looking at his impressive total for some time and gave a small nod of appreciation. The exercise had been worth the effort.

He went home after lunch, telling Sean and Krystyna that he had a mountain of paperwork to deal with and he needed peace and quiet in which to do so. Since neither Sean nor Krystyna had been making anything resembling a noise, they were left somewhat puzzled.

"What paperwork?" asked Sean, after Vince had left.

"He said something about invoices," Krystyna told him.

"I thought you dealt with all the invoices," Sean said.

"So did I," said Krystyna.

Vince continued to baffle his staff. On Wednesday, he announced that he would not be able to go to a meeting he had arranged. "I'm much too busy," he said, despite all evidence pointing to the contrary. He looked at Sean and said, "I can't send you. You're far too scruffy. I can't send Worzel Gummidge to meet my customers." He turned to Krystyna and surveyed her appearance. "You look moderately respectable, you'll have to go," he told her.

"Thank you for the flattery," Krystyna said, with a sourness that Vince either ignored or missed entirely.

Sean, who knew well enough not to attempt a response to the calumny that had befallen him, permitted himself a small smile. He had plenty of work to do and by concentrating on that, he could ignore Vince. Not that Vince seemed to be taking much notice of anybody. Sean did wonder, though not for long, what had got into his boss, but he'd seen this kind of thing before. Vince could turn a huff into a major project.

Just before midday, after Krystyna had departed for what was now her meeting, Sean returned from the toilet to find Vince embroiled in what appeared to be a less-than-friendly telephone conversation with an unknown person. As Sean knew very well, Vince did not like having to answer the phone, evidently viewing this as below the dignity and status of a manager.

"Well, I don't like *your* attitude, madam," Vince snarled into the receiver.

Sean could make out an animated female voice at the other end of the line. When it stopped for a moment, Vince took firm action.

"Go to hell, you witch," he shouted and slammed down the phone.

Sean weighed up the options and found that the scales were tipped heavily on the side of silence. He sat down and resumed his tussle with the website's fickle software. Within ten seconds, the telephone rang.

"Pick that up," Vince said gruffly.

Sean, who had been intending to do that very thing, lifted the receiver and said, "Good afternoon, Golf King."

There was a pause and then a woman's voice. "Oh, hello," she said. "I was on the phone to you a moment ago and some very rude man cut me off."

"Well, I can assure you that it wasn't me," Sean replied, wondering where this would lead.

"I know it wasn't you. You're not Scottish," she said.

"No, I'm not," Sean agreed.

Naturally, she was keen to know who had slammed the phone down on her. Sean, trusting that she was unaware of the numerical paucity of staff numbers at Golf King, professed ignorance.

"I'm terribly sorry," he said, "I just picked up the phone. I really couldn't say to whom you were speaking earlier. I can only apologise for—"

"It's not your fault," the woman told him. "But somebody needs to learn some manners. I wish to make a complaint in writing."

"Quite understandable," Sean said suavely. He allowed himself another little smirk while he told her to address the letter to Vince Kingmyle, Managing Director. He knew, though, that Vince would throw it into the bin and part of him wanted to tell her that, yes, this was the very same Vince Kingmyle that had shouted abuse at her a couple of minutes ago, but common sense suggested that this was, perhaps, a course of action akin to playing chicken on a very busy motorway.

"He never even said thanks. Just kept staring at his computer," Sean told Krystyna later. Vince had, predictably, finished early and left before Krystyna had returned.

Krystyna shook her head sympathetically. "He is becoming worse," she said. "He becomes ruder and ruder each day. Was he always so rude?"

"Not with the level of consistency he's reached now," Sean said. "Still, here's some good news – he's taken tomorrow and Friday off."

"Again," Krystyna observed.

"Well, he says he's got all this paperwork to do, but whatever it is he's doing, he won't be doing it in here."

"Maybe he will have calmed down by Monday," Krystyna suggested. "Or maybe he will not be here on Monday as well."

"He'll definitely be here on Monday," Sean said. "Monday is Laura day."

"Oh my God, of course" said Krystyna. "Oh, well, we have two days of freedom. What should we do with them?"

Sean considered the question for a few seconds. "Do you like playing Scrabble?" he asked.

Krystyna smiled enthusiastically. "Yes, oh, I like that game. It is so good for my English."

"Good," said Sean, "because we're not playing in Polish, I can assure you."

Chapter 23

The shock was almost enough to make Krystyna jump out of her black ankle boots. It was half past eight on a Monday morning and Vince was already at his desk. She knew the reason, of course. This was the first day at Golf King for the newest employee.

Laura Fotheringham arrived at ten o'clock. She was slender, had carefully frizzed and crimped blonde hair and an appearance of tallness. This was superficial, largely being due to the height of the shiny black stiletto heels she was wearing. The height of her heels was matched by the tightness of her pencil skirt, beneath which she wore black fishnet tights. She had not underdone either perfume or make-up.

Vince, who had raced to greet her when she arrived, dealt with the introductions. Laura neither spoke to, nor made eye contact, with Sean or Krystyna. Vince whisked her away to the small room where he had conducted the interviews.

Once they were alone, Sean ambled over to Krystyna's desk. "What do you make of that?" he asked.

Krystyna's face answered the question. "Who does she think she is?" she asked. "Royalty? And did you see him move? I never saw him move so quick."

"Vince has always seen himself as a man to charm women," Sean told her.

"I know," Krystyna said. "He used to ask me out to dinner and to go for a drink, but I always had something else to do."

Sean grinned. "Washing hair can take a very long time," he said.

Krystyna nodded. "Exactly. I do not find him charming. In fact, he gives me the creeps. I would rather go to dinner with a giant lizard."

Sean, who had heard similar sentiments from a few of his

former colleagues, could only agree. They took a tea break and speculated as to how long it would take Vince and Laura to emerge.

An hour later, the door opened. "Krystyna, can you make a cup of coffee for Laura. Nothing for me," Vince shouted across the office. The door closed again.

"What am I, a bloody skivvy?" muttered Krystyna. Sean was pleased to see that playing a few games of Scrabble had not undermined her English.

She returned from her mission with the look of someone who had been told to cleanse the Augean stables with a toothbrush. She said something under her breath. She spoke in Polish and Sean surmised, accurately, that it was a very rude word indeed.

"Madam does not want sugar. Madam wants a sweetener. Oh, madam does not want these sweeteners. Then what does he tell me? Only to go to the shops and find the sweeteners that she likes. My God, the woman has two legs."

Sean came over to her desk again, but Krystyna had not finished. "Oh yes, she has two legs and someone is making very sure that he gets a good look at them." She told Sean to get a chair and sit down at the end of her desk. She moved her own chair away from the table.

"So he is sitting there," she said, indicating Sean's position. She moved back a little further and crossed her legs, hitching up a trouser leg for effect. "And she is sitting like this, making sure that he gets a good look."

"Which he is no doubt doing," Sean said.

"Correct," said Krystyna. She narrowed her eyes and said, "He had better not expect me to dress like that, because there is no chance."

"He can't," Sean told her. "It's illegal. You could take him to court."

"You think he cares if it is illegal," Krystyna asked.

"No," Sean said, "but once he realises that he'd face a legal battle, he might think again."

"Might," Krystyna said. "That is the key word."

"At least your text-analysis skills are holding up," Sean told her. Krystyna was relieved to have the opportunity to smile about something.

Vince and Laura returned at quarter to one. It was a very brief return, as they left the office immediately. Vince said, "Going to lunch," and that was the last they saw of him for two hours. It was the last they saw of Laura for the day.

"I let her go early today," said Vince airily. "Only fair on your first day."

Sean glanced at Krystyna, whose face betrayed no emotion. Neither of them had been allowed the luxury of a short first day. Vince had one more bombshell.

"Krystyna, you'll need to move," he said. "Laura will be taking your desk. I will be working very closely with her and I need to have her sitting next to me."

Krystyna was hardly appalled at the prospect of not sitting beside Vince any longer. She said, "Okay," and began to move some things from her desk onto the empty desk next to Sean.

"Not there," Vince said. "Over there." He pointed to the solitary desk away from the bank of four desks that the team currently inhabited.

"Why not here?" Krystyna asked.

"Because I don't want you two sitting together," Vince said. "It will be a distraction if you're talking all the time."

"But we don't—" Krystyna began.

Vince cut her off with a glare. "That is what I have decided and that is what will happen," he said with finality. "Sean, you can help her set up her computer. I have to leave. I have a lot of work to do. Make sure that everything is ready for tomorrow. We are going to have some professionalism in this office."

Sean saw Krystyna make a move to speak, but caught her eye and shook his head. Vince left and Krystyna's frustration burst out. "Professionalism," she scoffed. "What would he know about professionalism?"

Sean leant back in his chair and sighed. "Don't know about you," he said, "but I can't see myself working here much longer. Actually, I might not have any choice. He gave me a contract for four months and that'll be up fairly soon and he hasn't said anything about renewing."

"What will you say if he does?" Krystyna asked.

"Probably tell him to stick it up his jacksey," Sean said.

Krystyna frowned and then brightened. "Jacksey is backside?" she said.

"Indeed," Sean confirmed. "Seven letters, 23 points plus 50 bonus for a seven-letter word."

Chapter 24

With the exception of a much-later arrival by Vince, Tuesday followed a similar template to Monday. Vince and Laura spent another two hours in the meeting room and left together to have lunch. Once again, Vince returned in mid-afternoon, having let Laura go home early.

"Parcel from Belgium for you," Krystyna said when Vince had deigned to return to the office. "I signed for it."

"Excellent," Vince replied, almost snatching it from her hand. He did not open it, but put it into his briefcase and prepared to leave. "I have to go," he said, and did.

"Belgium?" Sean said after Vince's departure.

Krystyna shrugged. "He had one last month also," she said. "From Belgium."

"Porn mags?" Sean suggested.

Krystyna laughed. "Who knows?" she said, feeling that she had reached a point where nothing Vince said or did could surprise her.

On Wednesday, Sean and Krystyna received an email from Vince in which he told them he would be working from home and that Laura would come and sit with them while they showed her what they did. This was met with the enthusiasm of a sailor about to walk the plank.

Not that Laura had arrived at work as yet. When she did, at ten past ten, she showed no signs of being interested in anything but her mobile phone. Neither Sean nor Krystyna went out of their way to instigate a meeting. Laura had, after all, received a copy of Vince's email and if she wanted to do something, that was up to her.

Eventually, she put down her phone and walked over to Sean's desk. Sean continued with what he was doing, expecting her to say something or to sit down beside him. Seconds passed. Finally, she did say something. "Why are you playing about on the internet when you're supposed to be at work?" she asked.

Sean pursed his lips and resisted the temptations – and dangers – of an immediate reply. He sat up straight and swivelled his chair slowly. Only then did he look at Laura. "This is the Golf King website," he said. "I am working on it, which is one of the things I get paid for."

There was no change in the stony expression on Laura's face. She waved a hand in the vague direction of where Krystyna was sorting out a bundle of post on the far side of the room. "And what about her, whatever her stupid name is, the Russian? What does she do, if anything?"

Sean was a more patient man than he was sometimes given credit for. Even so, he was unable to suppress the sigh that escaped him. He took a deep breath. "A few points," he said. "Her name is Krystyna, which is pronounced pretty much the same in any language. She is not Russian, she is Polish. I believe that Krystyna is a very common name in many countries. Czerniatynska, I couldn't really say, but I imagine that there are quite a lot of male Czerniatynskis and female Czerniatynskas in Poland and among the Polish diaspora throughout the world. Finally, she does rather a lot. She deals with the post, the emails, the phone calls, the bookings, meetings, travel, every bit of admin work you could imagine." He was tempted to add, *And quite a lot that you couldn't imagine.* Instead, he asked, "Does that answer your question?"

Laura merely gazed at him as if he were an unusual exhibit in a museum of natural history. It was uncertain that she had understood a great deal of what Sean had been saying. Finally, she said, "How can she do all that if she doesn't speak English properly?"

Sean pushed away the pair of scissors that were lying on his desk. They were offering too much temptation. "You will find," he said, as placidly as he could manage, "that Krystyna's English is very, very good. So good, in fact, that she is studying for a degree in English Literature. If that's not good enough for you, then—"

He got no further. Laura interrupted him. "Oh, I'm sorry," she said with sarcasm dripping from every word, "I didn't realise she was your girlfriend."

"She's not," Sean said, "though what relevance that has, I have no idea. Perhaps you should go and speak to her instead of hurling insults at somebody you know nothing about."

The conversation between Laura and Krystyna made Sean's encounter look like a raging success. Laura insisted on speaking very slowly, as if to a rather slow-witted infant. When Krystyna pointed out that she understood the English language perfectly well, Laura laughed at her. Krystyna walked away and was relieved to see that the clock had, apparently, sped up in sympathy with her predicament. Once Laura was out of earshot, she rushed across to Sean's desk. "I want to go out. No, not want. I need to go out," she said breathlessly. "Please come with me."

"I know what I want to do," Sean replied, "but it would put me in jail for several years. And yes, I will come out. I don't trust myself to be left alone with her."

Krystyna smiled. "You know what," she said, "I think we should have a Vince lunch hour."

Laura was coming back into the room as Sean replied, "You know what, I think you've had a very good idea."

"Let us go, then," Krystyna said. She favoured Laura with the broadest of smiles and said, "We are going to lunch. See you later."

"You can't," Laura said.

"Yes, we can," Sean contradicted her.

"What if the phone rings?" Laura demanded.

"Easy," Sean told her. "You pick up the receiver, listen through the top bit and speak into the bottom bit. You'll get the hang of it."

Chapter 25

Vince, whose relationship with his wife still had one or two icicles hanging from it, found himself at the centre of another conflict. Laura, already privileged enough to have Vince's mobile number, had telephoned him in the afternoon to provide him with the details, at least as she saw them, in a highly emotional and often tearful manner. Vince told her to take the rest of the week off. He would deal with the situation.

In many ways, he could have done without this. In another way, it gave him a surge of adrenaline. He was, after all, an experienced manager who had been compelled to deal with all sorts of unseemly states of affair during his days as a civil servant. He prided himself on his man-management skills, recalling a promotion interview where he was asked about his strengths and weaknesses. Among the vast list of strengths, he counted his ability to get the best out of people. It took some time before he reached the end of his strengths. As to weaknesses, he admitted to just one; he was a perfectionist and he acknowledged that he could be a little intolerant of those that did not share his ideals.

The fools had rejected him. Well, that was their loss, he thought as he got into his car. What was the motto? Ah, yes, the best managers for the best jobs. Vince had absolutely no doubt that he was the best manager and those idiots couldn't see it. Something like this, he thought, was irritating and annoying, but it was the sort of thing that happened in offices. People were different; they would not always see eye to eye. Good managers, though, could cope.

Even so, he felt a little uneasy. Despite what Laura had told him, he knew that Sean Monaghan was not a bully. Yes, he could be a bit prickly at times, but for the most part he was quiet, easy-going and very conscientious. True, he didn't suffer fools gladly

– come to think of it, he didn't suffer fools at all, but he was not a bully. Yes, he – Vince – would have to bring all his skills to the fore to solve this one and he remained deep in thought as he drove to the office.

His thought processes were interrupted only once. Some damned fool cyclist cut across him and he was forced to brake. "Clown," bellowed Vince as the cyclist made a crude gesture in his direction. Otherwise, his progress was smooth and he arrived a bit earlier than planned. He went for a walk. He wanted both Sean and Krystyna to be there where he arrived.

He must, he decided, be firm but fair. That was the way to manage and that was the way to nip this kind of thing in the bud. As soon as he removed his jacket, he told the pair of them that he wanted a meeting now. That meant now, this very moment. Without waiting for a reply, he strode off to the interview room.

Krystyna, whose desk was nearer to the room, set off, but Sean rushed up and caught her arm gently. He had been pretty certain that there would be fallout from the minor eruption and he said quietly, "Don't get angry or aggressive. It only makes him worse." Krystyna nodded.

Vince, who had made notes of the conversation with Laura, produced the charge sheet. Krystyna, who knew that Sean had a great deal more insight into the workings of Vince's mind, let her colleague act as counsel for the defence. Sean gave Vince the exact details of what Laura had said and how he had responded. Vince continued to take notes.

"How would you feel," asked Sean, "if someone came up to you and asked why you were playing about on the internet when you were supposed to be working? You can check it out for yourself. You have a look at the website and you'll see the work I did on it yesterday."

Vince finished another note and looked up. "A misunderstanding," he said. "That's all." Seeing the sceptical look on Sean's face, he felt the need to expound his theory. "But I agree.

She was a bit tactless. She could have asked what you were doing. I'll speak to her."

Sean felt slightly mollified, though only slightly. "And what about what she said about Krystyna? That was plain offensive. In fact, I'd call it racist."

Vince sucked in his breath. "Well," he said hesitantly, "I think you're going a bit far, but yes, I can see how some people might take offence."

"Some people?" asked Sean with incredulity.

"Let me finish," said Vince, in a surprisingly conciliatory tone. "Don't forget she's young, and sometimes younger people say things they don't really mean. She probably meant it as a joke, but not everyone has the same sense of humour."

Sean wasn't buying it. "So if I said that everybody from Poland was really thick and really lazy, that would be a joke?" he said.

Vince didn't want to go deeper into this particular pool. "I'll talk to her," he said, avoiding the question. He didn't feel comfortable getting into the machinations of linguistics with somebody like Sean and turned to Krystyna instead.

"Did you feel offended?" Vince asked her.

"I did not hear that conversation," Krystyna said, "but when she spoke to me, she talked to me like I was a very small child. Every word she said v-e-r-y s-l-o-w-l-y like I was simple."

Vince grimaced. "I'm sure she meant no offence," he said cheerfully. He looked across with an optimistic smile and saw, from the stern faces looking back at him, that they were far from sure. He decided that he was on firmer ground when it came to leaving the office at lunchtime.

"You shouldn't have left her on her own," he said.

"I suppose not," Sean conceded, "but to be honest, we'd both had enough of being insulted. Anyway, we only went out for a cup of coffee. We weren't gone for that long and by the time we'd got back, she'd disappeared."

"She told me that the phone never stopped ringing," Vince said.

Krystyna almost laughed, but held herself back. "I would be surprised," she said. "It hardly rang all day. Anyway, it is not difficult to say that someone will call you back."

Vince pursed his lips. He knew that what they were telling him had a distinct ring of truth about it. He made a few more notes and said, "Okay, you know my feelings. We don't all have to like each other, we just have to work together. I'll have a word with her, but I don't want anyone getting upset. We have to get along professionally, even if we don't personally." He sat back with an air of finality. "Anything else?" he asked.

Sean would have liked to have said a great deal more, but knew that it would be strategically sensible to leave things as they were. He couldn't, though, resist one final question. "What exactly is Laura's job title?" he asked.

"Head of Marketing," said Vince.

Sean stared at him expressionlessly. He did not risk glancing at Krystyna. The meeting came to an end and Vince announced that he had another meeting to go to. He would be back later, he said.

"Well?" Krystyna asked when he'd gone.

Sean shook his head. "He believed what we said," he told her.

"So he should. It was true," Krystyna replied.

"Doesn't always work like that," Sean said. They sat in silent contemplation for a few seconds. "Head of Marketing," Sean said with derision. "Now that *is* a joke."

Chapter 26

Vince was so content with his arbitration and conciliation skills that he took Friday off, reassured by the fact that he had handled everything in a masterly fashion. Besides, Laura would not be there, so there could be no repeat of Wednesday's problems. He would talk to her on Monday and everything would run smoothly from now on.

While that may have been the case in his professional life, his personal life still had uncomfortable undulations. Valerie had also taken the day off and for once, Victoria was up early. Vince found himself enduring a breakfast so quiet that it would have met with approval from the head of a Trappist monastery.

He consoled himself that this form of mental torture could only last for so long. In the case of the present day, it would only last for a few more minutes. His daughter's startlingly early rise from bed was down to the fact that she and Valerie were going shopping. Vince would be left with a more acceptable form of peace.

Once his sullen wife and even more sullen daughter had left, he felt more comfortable. He collected his golf clubs and put them in his car, then went to the spare room. There were papers that needed to be sorted out, but he had done the bulk of the work earlier in the week. He allowed himself a tight smile. No doubt, he thought, that those two members of the awkward squad in his office thought his claims of working at home were fanciful. Not so, he knew, and this proved it. He had done a lot of work and he – and the business – would reap the rewards of his labours.

He left the house with two envelopes that needed to be posted and drove to the golf course via the post office. That was his work done for the day and he arrived at the course at the same time as another club member, Gary Thornley, a young man that

Vince knew from his days as a civil servant.

"Hey, Vince, how's it going?" Gary asked.

"Couldn't be better," Vince responded. He liked Gary. For one thing, he supported the right team and for another, he showed Vince the respect that he, Vince, felt he deserved. Too many of the younger fellows were, in his opinion, just a bit too cocky and full of themselves. Gary, though, was the sort to give due deference to those who, like Vince, had achieved something in their lives.

Vince invited Gary to join him on the course. Gary agreed and they set off. It was a fine day, though there was a stiff breeze.

"Bit gusty," Gary noted.

"Minor hazard," Vince said with a superior smile. "Nothing compared to what I had at Troon a few weeks ago. Wind blasting in off the Irish Sea, squally showers. Proper links golf. That separates the men from the boys."

As they progressed, Vince provided a shot by shot of his outstanding round in Ayrshire. Nothing was overlooked. It was important, Vince felt, to cover everything. Without the small details, the large picture could not be drawn. Gary, who had not had the pleasure of accompanying Vince on a round before, began to feel his energy draining. He felt almost relieved when he sliced a drive into some heavy rough, but even that provided little respite. As they searched for his ball, Vince was reminded of a similar position he had found himself in during that round at Troon and felt obliged to give Gary a full and detailed description of the type of grass, the lie, the position of the green, the location of the flag, the way he had addressed the problem, the club he had used and the shot he had played. The latter, of course, had been something of a miracle and Gary was left with the impression that only Severiano Ballesteros at his most inspired could have matched what Vince had achieved.

What Gary did find interesting – and he had struggled thus far – was that Vince did not appear to have any special talent on the course. He was quite clearly a decent enough player, but there was nothing in what he had done thus far to suggest that he was anything beyond a reasonably competent club player.

"Just can't seem to find my rhythm today," Vince said, as if reading Gary's thoughts.

"Not sure I ever do," Gary replied with commendable modesty.

"Perhaps it's because I've had such a hard week," Vince mused.

Gary was not certain that he wanted to know, but was pretty sure he was going to find out. "How's it going, the golf-tourism business, then?" he asked.

"Mobbed," Vince told him. "I've had to employ extra staff. It's going to get even bigger. I've got a marketing expert in."

"Oh," Gary said, trying to maintain some enthusiasm. "Where did you get him from?"

"Her," Vince corrected him. "She's young, but dynamic. Full of ideas of how to get our name out there. That's what she's there for, really. She gets the ideas and some are good, some are bad. Then it's down to me to make decisions. Sort out the wheat from the chaff. That's the way things work. You need people with ideas, but you have to rein in their enthusiasm sometimes. Nothing wrong with enthusiasm, of course. It just needs to be channelled."

Gary, whose own enthusiasm was waning by the minute, could only nod in agreement. Vince, however, powered on. "The next big thing is tours abroad. I've got plenty of contacts. America, Spain, Portugal, we can expand into those areas." Suddenly, he stopped and stared at Gary. Gary glanced round, unsure of what he'd done. Vince clapped him on the shoulder with some vigour.

"That's it," he said, "I've got it."

"What is it?" asked Gary with some trepidation.

"What I'm going to do," said Vince, "is create a new company. Golf King Tours, I think. Yes, that sounds good. Golf King Tours.

Keep the overseas business apart from the home business."

Vince was unstoppable now and Gary felt as though he was being overwhelmed by two strong winds coming from different directions.

"I may be officially on a day off," Vince said, "but a good businessman never rests, never stops thinking. I've got staff in my office, they're good at what they do, but they don't have the imagination. That's where the difference lies. They'll be sitting there thinking, oh yeah, it's Friday and that idler Vince is out there playing golf. But they never see beyond that. Why? Because they don't have what it takes."

Gary could do little more than nod now. He looked at his watch and then at his scorecard. It was almost two o'clock and they had only completed nine holes. Already, it felt like a long day and for once, he began to feel a little envious of those who had been condemned to spending their Friday sitting in an office.

Chapter 27

It was unlikely that Sean and Krystyna would have cared a great deal that they were being condemned for lack of imagination on the one hand and envied for their comfortable office life on the other. Sean was much more interested in the discovery he had made. "Come and look at this," he said to Krystyna.

Krystyna sat down and looked at the monitor. She read down the page of the document that Sean had found and looked at him. "Where did you find that?" she asked.

"The Great Leader saved it to the shared drive," he explained.

"So that is our new Head of Marketing," Krystyna said.

"And doesn't she just have the experience we need?" Sean asked.

The document that Vince had copied to the wrong drive was the CV of Laura Fotheringham. Sean and Krystyna learned that Laura had left school at the earliest possible age and had managed to pass, though only just, two of her GCSE exams. She had worked as a trainee hairdresser, though that appeared to be an unfulfilled vocation, after which she had been employed by two supermarkets and an insurance company, for whom she had worked in a call centre. Nowhere in the document did the word 'marketing' appear.

Krystyna looked worried for more than one reason. "He will not know that you opened it?" she asked.

Sean shook his head. "I took a copy of it," he told her. "It was obvious what it was, so I copied it to my computer and opened it. I'll delete it later."

Krystyna sighed. "I cannot believe this," she said. "She will never be able to do this job. Why did Vince employ somebody like this?" She stopped, realising that she knew the answer to her own question.

As noon approached, they had a visitor.

"Thought I'd come and see you on your last day of freedom," Carol Whelan said as Krystyna showed her into the office.

"Thank you for reminding me," Krystyna replied. She made Carol a cup of tea and then told Sean to show Carol the infamous CV.

"Good luck with that one," Carol said after she had seen the grim evidence.

"She's been employed here for a week and she's spent roughly six hours in the office," Sean said. "Monday and Tuesday, she was in there with The Best Manager, Wednesday she got the huff and did a runner, Thursday and today she's off because she needed time to recover from all the bullying that she suffered."

"You are cruel, heartless people," Carol said. "I expect it from a gangland thug like you," she said, slapping Sean with her newspaper, "but not from you, Krystyna. You have an evil dark side to your character."

"I know," Krystyna admitted. "Actually, I am a witch. But please do not tell anyone."

"Don't worry," Carol said. "I'm one as well. Vince says so."

"It must be true, then," Krystyna agreed.

Defiantly flouting regulations, Sean locked the office and joined Carol and Krystyna for lunch. The week ahead was not an appealing proposition, so there was no harm, thought Sean, in enjoying what remained of this week.

"Personality clash, I think," Krystyna said as she recalled her first encounter with Laura.

"You mean you've got a personality and she hasn't?" Carol said. "I have the same problem with Lord Kingmyle. How long do you think she's going to last?"

"Depends on how long it takes Vince to realise she's useless," Sean said. "Mind you, surely even he must have had a fair idea. He's read her CV."

"And left it conveniently for everyone else to read," Carol said.

"It's ever since he met that American fellow, Carl what's-his-name. He's the sort who's going to have a building full of busty blondes wearing minimal clothing."

Krystyna laughed. "Laura is not even busty," she said. "She is so thin."

"I suppose he has to start somewhere," Carol said. "Got you bikini ready?" she asked Krystyna.

Krystyna pulled a face. "If he tells me to start wearing – what was it – minimal clothing, then he is going to get a surprise." She grinned maliciously. "I will crack his bald head like an egg."

Carol smiled. "I said you were evil," she said.

Sean fumbled in his pocket and took out a piece of paper. "When you were talking about witches earlier on, I remembered this," he said, passing the sheet to Carol.

Carol put it on the table so that Krystyna could see it as well.

Looking for a break? Then ditch the witch and join a Golf King tour. The perfect opportunity to play a round.

Sean sat back to await the reaction. Carol and Krystyna looked at each other and then at Sean. Neither of them said a word.

"Vince's idea of an advert for golf magazines," he explained, as Carol slowly lowered her head on to the table and gently banged her forehead a few times. Krystyna had closed her eyes and was shaking her head.

"Surely to God he hasn't?" Carol said.

"I managed to dissuade him," Sean told her. "I said to him, 'you can't put that out' and all he said was 'why not?' and I had to point out that it was just a tad on the sexist side and that it made it sound like he was running a brothel. Then I made the mistake of saying that all it would generate would be negative publicity and he thought that would be great. He said that if we got lots of publicity, it didn't matter whether it was good or bad. Anyway, I started on about advertising standards and other legal stuff and just about managed to make him realise that it wasn't a good idea."

"You're a feminist hero,'" said Carol, patting his hand.

"Still, he's got an experienced and talented Head of Marketing now, so there'll be no problems with adverts from now on," Sean said.

Krystyna had just about recovered from her first view of Vince's intended advert. "Do you think that she is capable of having an idea?" she asked.

"Highly unlikely," Sean said. "It should be interesting, though."

"Interesting does not, of course, mean enjoyable," Carol warned.

Chapter 28

Vince Kingmyle was not a man to be beset by self-doubt and by midday on Monday morning, he was fully confident that his office was a happy place for everyone. He had spent three hours with Laura, assuring her that she was a person of paramount importance to the organisation. To prove this, he intended to take her to all of the meetings that he had arranged for the week ahead. There were meetings with clients, visits to hotels and discussions with travel agents. It was a busy time and he told her that her experience and knowledge would be invaluable.

What Vince overlooked was the minor detail that his office was now, effectively, split into two camps, between which there was little interaction. Vince had only fleeting contact with Sean and Krystyna. In many ways, they were happy with this arrangement. The less interference, the better, was Sean's view and in some ways, it was a tribute to their abilities that they needed no supervision as they went about their jobs.

If Vince's dealings with Sean and Krystyna were on the thin side, Laura's were positively anorexic. She had done little more than shrug when Vince had suggested that she might be a shade more diplomatic when approaching people. Happy in the knowledge that she was in a position far senior to that of the pair of them, she decided that ignoring them altogether would be the best policy. Not that Sean and Krystyna were in any way disappointed by this outlook.

It followed that Vince and Laura spent little time in the office during the week. During one of their absences, Sean wandered across to Krystyna's remote outpost on the far side of the office.

"How are things in the leper colony?" he asked.

"Oh, I like it here," Krystyna told him. "It is peaceful. And it is not a leper colony. It is a very beautiful desert island."

Sean could see her point. "I'm quite envious," he said. "You don't have to listen to those two gibbering away for hours."

"What do they talk about?" Krystyna asked.

"Television, mostly," Sean said. "If I stay here much longer, I'll know everything that's happened in every soap opera and reality show that's going."

Krystyna frowned. "I do not understand why they call it reality," she said. "If that is reality, I think I prefer to live in a different world."

Sean could only agree. "If I want to spend my time looking at dysfunctional idiots, then I just come to this office."

Krystyna laughed. "You include me?" she asked.

"Of course not," Sean said. "I might buy some earplugs, though with any luck, they'll be out and about all the time, dispensing pearls of wisdom alongside their Managing Director and Head of Marketing business cards."

"Where are they now?" Krystyna asked, as Vince did not see the need to disclose his whereabouts to her these days.

"Some flashy golf hotel near Perth," Sean told her. "Just as well he gave her a lift or she'd have probably booked a flight to Western Australia."

By Friday, Vince and Laura had exhausted their hectic schedule of meetings and were back in the office. Here, they were merely exhausting Sean, who had to spend two hours or so listening to the latest goings on in the world of popular television entertainment. It continued into his lunch break and he felt the need to inhale some fresh air, or at least a few fresh car fumes.

As he got up to leave, Vince could not resist a passing comment. "Of course, Sean looks down on the sort of things that everybody else likes," he smirked.

Sean raised an eyebrow. "Everybody?" he said.

"Come on," Vince said, "shows that millions of people watch rather than those arty-farty things on BBC4 that only you and Carol watch. The rest of us have to pay our licence fees just so you can watch that stuff."

Sean was not in the mood to be wound up by Vince and was more than happy to leave it there, but to his surprise, Laura chipped in.

"What is it you don't like about those programmes?" she demanded.

"Apart from the fact that they're witless rubbish?" Sean asked, before answering his own question. "It's mindless piffle and I don't understand why anybody gets so caught up in them. You can't live your life vicariously." He waited a moment for a response, but none arrived. Having said all he wanted to say, he went out for a walk.

Vince and Laura looked at one another querulously. "Why would I want to be a vicar?" Vince asked her.

Laura, whose failure to comprehend was equal to, if not greater than, that of her boss, shook her head. "There's something weird about him," she said. "He's not normal."

Vince, who attributed Sean's unconventional tastes to the malign influence of Carol Whelan, adopted a surprisingly liberal and phlegmatic stance. "He's just a bit different," he said. "Takes all sorts to make a world."

Chapter 29

Vince, who had a great passion for lists, had compiled a three-page document detailing a training plan for Laura. He emailed this to her, with copies for Sean and Krystyna. There were instructions for Sean to show Laura the IT systems and documents. Part of Krystyna's brief, which was considerable, was to forward any emails that she received, so that Laura could see how the business ran.

Laura did not take a great deal of interest in the training. She sat with Sean while he talked about folders, shared drives, documents, spreadsheets, websites and lots of other things that bored her. Her mobile phone was, evidently, a much more pleasurable diversion. She took no notes and walked away without a word when Sean had finished.

Krystyna was afforded equally little attention. Laura yawned ostentatiously as Krystyna told her about phone calls, emails, spreadsheet maintenance, time recording, invoices, stationery ordering and booking travel and hotels. What, she wondered, had any of this to do with her? She was Head of Marketing, not some idiot of a pen-pusher. What did she care if the number of staples was getting low?

Vince did not play any further part in the training, though he instructed Laura to send him any emails that looked interesting and might need his attention. This was a source of some irritation to Laura, who had intended to delete the emails without even looking at them. She felt this to be rather demeaning work for somebody of her importance, but imagined that it would only be necessary for a short while.

She found that most of the correspondence received by Krystyna was rather banal, though there were one or two that seemed to be promising in terms of future business. One of these came from a golf-club secretary, who had telephoned to express interest in the operations of Golf King and suggested that there could be mutual benefits for both his golf club and the company. Krystyna had put everything into an email and Laura decided that Vince should see this, though she made some amendments to the document before sending it on. She considered, for a moment, telling Krystyna that she should take more care over her use of English, but decided against it. The stupid woman would be unlikely to understand.

Vince was interested. He was about to dial the number of the Club Secretary, but changed his mind. "I think I'll pay them a visit," he told Laura. "Tynemouth isn't that far. Straight down the A1 and back. I can get there in under two hours. I'll have a look at the place first. Get there early, have a round and check the place out."

With no meetings arranged for the following day, Vince took the road south. Living east of Edinburgh was a help, as he was able to hit the main road without battling against and with the bulk of commuter traffic. He arrived in Tynemouth earlier than he'd expected and found the golf club. It was not, he thought, the most imposing place he had seen, but he was here now and he may as well get out on the course.

It was, he felt, a bit of a disappointing course, certainly by comparison with what he was used to playing in Scotland. There were few people around and he putted out on the final hole and headed for the clubhouse. He would have some lunch and then see if the secretary was around. Now that he'd come all this way, he probably ought to see if he could have a chat.

After lunch, Vince wandered around and found a man wearing a club blazer and tie. "Could you tell me if the Club Secretary is here today?" Vince asked him.

"He certainly is," the man replied. "You're looking at him."

"Mr Appleyard," Vince said, holding out his hand in greeting, "Vince Kingmyle."

The secretary shook Vince's hand, but puzzlement was all

over his face. "I'm Bill Robson," he said.

Now Vince was baffled. "Who is Graham Appleyard?" he asked.

Bill Robson shook his head. "No idea," he admitted. "Never heard of him."

Vince frowned. "How long have you been Club Secretary?" he asked.

"Eight years," Bill said.

Vince reached into his jacket pocket and produced the email that Laura had forwarded. He showed it to Bill Robson and said, "I don't understand. It says here, Graham Appleyard, Club Secretary of Tynemouth Golf Club."

"I can see what it says," Bill said, "but whoever Graham Appleyard is, he isn't me."

Vince, for want of anywhere else to look, stared at the ceiling. Bill regarded him for a few moments and then had an idea.

"Come with me," he said. He led Vince to a small office and pulled a large green book from a shelf. "Even I couldn't tell you the name of every member," he said.

The membership list failed to provide any evidence of a man called Appleyard, Graham or otherwise. Bill Robson closed the book and looked at Vince. "Can't explain," he said. "Unless someone's playing a practical joke on you."

Vince walked back to the bar and ordered a mineral water. He was half-tempted to have something stronger, but his last experience of alcohol had not been pleasant in any way. There was nothing he could do except...then he remembered. There was a telephone number. Vince took out his phone and dialled.

"Hello?"

"Is that Graham Appleyard?" asked Vince.

"It is," came the reply.

"My name is Vince Kingmyle," said Vince, playing it neutral for the moment.

There was a brief silence. "Oh, the golf tours man," said

Graham Appleyard.

"Correct," said Vince. "Could I ask where you are?"

"Where am I?" repeated Graham. "I'm at the golf club."

"What golf club?" Vince asked.

"My golf club," Graham said.

Vince pursed his lips. "Not Tynemouth," he said.

"Teignmouth," Graham said, "not Tynemouth."

"Where's Teignmouth?" asked Vince blankly.

"Devon," said Graham cheerfully. "About halfway between Exeter and Torquay."

Vince held out his phone and stared at it. He felt like throwing it across the room, but eventually brought it back to his ear. "Oh, right, thank you. I'll be in touch."

He rang off and put his phone on the table as softly as he could manage. He sat there for several seconds and muttered to himself. "Right. I am going to kill her."

It was early enough to get back to the office and the traffic was fairly quiet. Vince drove with a face that suggested to any passing motorist that it would not be the best idea to get in his way. Hundreds of thoughts battled for possession of his head. All of them involved Krystyna. He would sack her. Then he wouldn't. Then he would. A final warning.

By the time he arrive back at the office, he was still undecided. He would see what she had to say. He waited outside the front door for a few seconds to compose himself before he entered. All three of his staff were still at their desks.

Vince did not speak and marched to Krystyna's desk. He slammed down the printed email and said, "I suppose this is your idea of a joke. Polish humour, was it?"

Krystyna looked blankly at him. She looked at the email and said, "What do you mean?"

Vince said, "I have been to Northumberland. The golf club is in Devon. You got the wrong place and you sent me to the wrong club."

Krystyna was none the wiser. "I did not send you anywhere," she said.

Vince's temper was not helped by Krystyna's mild replies. "You took the phone call, yes or no?" he demanded, his voice rising. "You wrote this email, yes or no?"

"Wait," said Krystyna. She looked back through her sent items and found what she was looking for. She opened the email she had sent to Laura, sat back in her chair and pointed at the screen. "There," she said.

Vince looked at the email on the screen and the printed email on the table. Krystyna's original had 'Teignmouth'. The one sent by Laura said 'Tynemouth'.

"You didn't change it?" asked Vince quietly.

"No," said Krystyna. "I remember, I asked the man how to spell it because I said, 'Sorry, I am Polish, I have never heard of this place and can you spell it for me?' and he was very nice, he laughed and said not to worry because most English people cannot spell it, either."

"Or Scottish," muttered Vince. "Print that email," he added.

Krystyna decide that silence was a good option and printed the document.

"Right," said Vince, his mouth tightening ominously. He walked across the room to Laura's desk. Laura had been smirking at the evident discomfort of Krystyna, but was now keeping a straight face and staring at her computer.

Vince put the two emails on her desk. "Did you change that?" he asked.

Laura looked at the sheets and said, "Of course I did."

"Why?" demanded Vince.

"Because she's stupid," Laura told him. "She spelled Tynemouth wrong."

"She spelled Teignmouth right, though," Vince said. "Teignmouth in Devon."

Laura opened her mouth, but closed it again before any sound could escape. She opened it again, but this time, Vince pre-empted her.

"Do not say anything," he said darkly. "I am going home now. I will speak to you about this in the morning."

Even Laura realised that attempting to stage a defence was not, at this juncture, the best of moves. She sat in silence as Vince turned and walked out. Then she fired a look of sheer hatred at Krystyna before making her own exit.

Krystyna, wearing a wry smile, came across to Sean's desk. "Does Vince ever apologise for anything?" she asked.

"No," Sean said. "I think he sees it as a sign of weakness. Anyway, what was all that about? I caught some of it."

Krystyna explained. By the time she had finished, the office of Golf King Ltd was filled with the sound of hysterical giggling.

Chapter 30

Vince spent part of his evening planning the discussion that he would have with Laura the following morning. Unfortunately for him, the following day was a Friday and Laura saw this as the ideal time to develop a cold. She even took the trouble to get up early so that she could phone before Vince got to the office. She knew that there was a fair chance that Krystyna would be the only person there, but she was not planning to have a long conversation.

"Won't be in, got a cold," she said when Krystyna answered.

"Oh," Krystyna said and the line went dead.

Sean arrived half an hour later and learned of the medical situation.

"She's not terribly original, is she?" he said.

A similar thought occurred to Vince when Krystyna gave him the news, though it was expressed in rather more florid terms. He unlocked his cupboard and placed his notes in a folder marked 'Laura Fotheringham'. He felt that he was being made to look foolish and considered giving up and retiring to the golf course, but the sky was grey and would soon unload a torrent of water. He discounted the idea and stared morosely at his computer.

He decided to have a look at the Golf King website and discovered that Sean had made some changes and improvements to it. There were more menus, more detailed information and the graphics looked better. Feeling more charitable, he said, "Our website looks pretty good now."

Sean looked up, somewhat taken aback at receiving something that faintly smacked of praise. "Took me ages to work out how to get those menus like that," he said, more for the sake of making a response than because he felt a need to say it.

"Grand job," Vince said, magnanimity coursing through his system. He got up and walked over to Krystyna's desk. "How are you getting on with the travel agents?" he asked. He had given Krystyna a list of agents to contact and had designed a form and check list himself to facilitate this.

"Only two more to do," Krystyna said a little nervously.

"You're doing a grand job," Vince told her. He looked outside and announced that he was going to go out before the rain fell, but that he would be back by lunchtime.

"What's up with Doctor Feelgood?" Sean asked Krystyna once Vince had gone. "All I've been hearing is 'grand job' this morning."

"Maybe he feels guilty," she suggested.

"Can't say I was aware that he had a conscience," Sean said. "It makes me uneasy when he starts being nice."

Krystyna agreed. "Do you think he wants us to do something?" she asked.

"Could be," Sean said. "I wonder what he's going to do about Problem Child."

Krystyna pulled a face. "Oh, she will flash her legs at him and he will love her again," she said.

Sean wasn't so sure. "She can't go on like this, though. She comes in late every day, she goes home early every day, assuming she comes in at all and when she is here, she either does nothing or she annoys either you or me and usually both of us. In fact, I'd say she's more productive when she's not here because she's not in the way."

"I wanted to tell him that she always goes early," Krystyna said, "but he likes her so much that I thought he will get angry with me."

"I know," Sean agreed. "Actually, I should have said something. He knows me better than he knows you, so I should have spoken to him, but I chickened out."

Krystyna smiled sympathetically. "It is not your fault," she said. "She is useless and Vince is blind to that because he thinks she is so wonderful. Perhaps he will see now." She frowned, as

Sean was staring at the ceiling and did not appear to be listening.

Sean curtailed his inspection of the ceiling and looked at Krystyna. "I've got an idea," he said quietly, as though there were listening devices throughout the room. He gave her a hurried rundown of his plan and she nodded thoughtfully.

"We'll do it next week," he said. "Can't tell which day yet."

"It is worth a try," Krystyna agreed.

Vince came back with a stealth that belied his rather overweight appearance and found the pair still in conversation. His bonhomie, however, had not deserted him.

"What are you two conspiring about?" he asked cheerfully.

"Just the overthrow of tyrannical governments," Sean said insouciantly.

Vince smiled benevolently and devoted himself to catching up on the news as presented by *The Sun*. It was, after all, Friday and he saw no reason to exert himself. He even allowed Sean and Krystyna to go out at the same time and also encouraged them to take their time. "The answerphone can cope if things get busy," he told them.

"What *is* wrong with him?" Krystyna whispered when they were some way down the road.

"I don't know, but it's disconcerting," Sean said. "He's got something up his sleeve." For now, though, Sean had a plan of his own and dragged Krystyna off to her favourite coffee shop to discuss it further.

Chapter 31

Vince took great pride in the knowledge and wisdom he had accumulated in his long career in management. One of his favourite mantras concerned the need for a good work-life balance and at present, he felt his own to be somewhat out of kilter. In fact, he felt as if it was being dictated to by a malfunctioning see-saw.

Just when he felt that everything was functioning perfectly in the world of Golf King Ltd, his domestic life had descended into a maelstrom. That this maelstrom was one largely of his own making rather bypassed Vince, who lay the blame squarely on the shoulders of his daughter and, to a lesser degree, those of Stuart Webster, from whom he had heard nothing since the ill-fated Friday night trip that had started the descent.

It had taken him time and patience to get things back to something approaching normality, but Vince regarded himself as a man of near-infinite patience and now, at least, he was being treated with a degree of civility by both his wife and his daughter. Victoria had gone so far as to find a job, working in a shop selling cosmetics. While Vince would have preferred to see a little more ambition, there was considerably less likelihood of her straying into morally dubious territory, particularly as the shop was located in the rarefied air of Morningside rather than the fleshpots of Leith.

The see-saw had, of course, not stayed level for long and now Vince had the problem of Laura to sort out. He wondered if the problems were merely those of teething rather than more deep-rooted, but he was not entirely sure. He was quick to shake off any uncertainties and told himself that his managerial skills would win out. He had come across plenty of awkward types in the Civil Service – indeed, the whole institution seemed to be a dumping ground for the lazy, the incompetent, the inept and the unemployable at times – but he had always triumphed, at least in his own eyes.

With a determination to resolve things quickly, he arrived earlier than usual on Monday morning. It was another hour or so before Laura arrived and Vince allowed her the time to get herself some coffee before taking her into the private room that served so many purposes. This particular meeting did not take on the cosy aspect of the last two occasions in which he had spoken to her.

Vince was a man whose views could be described as being closer to the reactionary than the revolutionary. Even he, though, was a little uneasy at some of the opinions aired by his Head of Marketing, in whom he had placed such faith. He decided to let her speak at some length before giving his own insights.

As Vince laid another A4 pad to waste, Laura went on at some length. The mix up over the golf clubs of Tynemouth and Teignmouth was, she insisted, entirely the fault of Krystyna. Furthermore, Krystyna was always getting things wrong, but that was to be expected. She was a foreigner and what could foreigners know about English? Laura found it strange that a Scottish company specialising in that most Scottish of games, golf, employed people who were not Scottish. She also let it be known that the two 'foreigners' were in league with each other and conspiring to make her, Laura, feel unwanted and isolated.

She said a great deal more, and as she assassinated Sean and Krystyna in character form, Vince went on writing. Eventually, the tirade came to an end and Vince stared at the growing pile of paper that lay in front of him and wondered where to start.

He tried to concentrate on the specific problem of the confusion of the golf clubs. He tried to make Laura see that it was, in fact, her mistake. He was, he said, not a man who would crucify somebody for making a mistake. He would, though, like her to acknowledge that she had been at fault. Laura would not give such an acknowledgement, preferring to point a damning finger in the direction of Krystyna. The woman was, she insisted, incompetent.

Vince sighed. This was more awkward than he had expected. He defended Krystyna in terms that would have made the young Pole blush had she been party to the remarks. He also rode to the rescue of the character and personality of Sean, though the latter would, no doubt, have regarded some of the compliments as somewhat backhanded.

And so it went on. Vince began to feel as if he were engaged in a never-ending game of tennis as Laura returned all of his serves with equal ferocity. There appeared to be no possibility of a tie break, but Vince was nothing if not persistent. The meeting dragged on and on with no sign of a breakthrough. In the end, Vince could only resort to the power of his position. He was the man in charge, his decision was final and if people didn't like that, then they could go and earn a living elsewhere.

More than three hours after she had entered the room, Laura walked out and marched past firstly Krystyna and then Sean. She said nothing and made no eye contact. Sean and Krystyna did, though they made no comment, either. Vince was still around and any discussion could only happen once he was out of the building.

Vince had remained in the meeting room. He leant heavily on the table and sighed. It had not been a raging success and he was irritated. What had seemed such a good idea a few weeks ago seemed – what was that phrase that Sean liked? Oh yes – a bit rubbish now. Vince shook his head. A bit rubbish? He wondered where Sean had picked that one up and then the image of Carol Whelan came into his head. "Wonder where he picked that one up, as well," he muttered. He gathered up his notes and slipped them into a transparent plastic cover. He felt decidedly vexed, but above all, he was hungry.

He left the room, closing the door very quietly so as not to betray his feelings. Calmly, he walked to his desk and locked away the notes he had taken. With as much cheeriness as he could muster, he said, "Lunch," and walked out with an air of jauntiness that belied his true emotions.

Sean wasn't falling for it. "The bomb could go off soon," he told Krystyna.

"Let us hope the magic mushrooms are strong," she said.

Chapter 32

The relocation of relations between Vince and Laura to somewhere north of the Arctic Circle was good news for one person. Sean was able to concentrate on his work and managed to get over his disappointment at not being kept up to date with popular culture.

The opportunity that he was seeking, and which he had discussed with Krystyna, was not long in arriving. Krystyna, who always dealt with the post, sent him an email one morning telling him that there was a parcel from Belgium for Vince. Sean told her to keep hold of it.

"Can you come and help me with a spreadsheet?" Krystyna asked Sean a few minutes later.

"Yeah, no problem," Sean replied, fully aware that spreadsheets were not going to be the centre of interest. As he got up, he noticed Laura glance up and sneer.

"I checked his diary," Sean whispered as he sat down at Krystyna's desk. "Looks like he's here all day today, but he's got a meeting at eleven tomorrow. It's up the West End, so he's bound to come in here and I reckon that'll be it for the day."

"What if he is looking for the parcel?" Krystyna asked. "He will have the tracking number and it will say it has been delivered."

"Couriers get things wrong," Sean told her. "I was waiting for a parcel once – from Belgium, oddly enough – and the Belgian Post website said it had been delivered at 17:15 on Monday evening. Well, I didn't have it and I spent half of Tuesday trying to find out who was supposed to be delivering it in the UK. I went to the post office to see if it had been left there and they told me to ring Royal Mail. I rang Royal Mail and they told me the reference was a Parcel Force one, so I rang Parcel Force. They told me it was nothing to do with them, so I didn't have a clue who was meant to be delivering this thing. I'd pretty much given up for the day when a van turned up and there was my delivery, more a less a day to the minute later than the Belgian Post site said."

Krystyna couldn't resist asking what was in the parcel.

"Beer," Sean told her, "so it wasn't like it was trivial."

Krystyna smiled. "I think we can say that this is not beer."

"Safe assumption," Sean agreed. "So if he does start asking where it is, just tell him they said it's been delivered and that it hasn't and that you'll ring them up and sort it out. He'll never phone them himself."

When he got back to his own desk, Vince looked up and asked, "Problem fixed?"

"Completely," Sean said truthfully. "Excel does some weird things," he added, which was also truthful, but irrelevant to the present situation.

As he had anticipated, Vince remained in the office until late afternoon.

The following day, a Thursday, was the day of Vince's latest meeting. As Vince prepared to leave, Sean decided to give his plan a little impetus. "Will you be back today?" he asked casually.

"No," Vince said shortly. "Why, did you need to see me about something?"

Sean produced the answer he'd prepared earlier. "I wanted to have a chat about the website sometime," he said. "I had a couple of ideas, but I wanted to see what you thought."

Vince liked website enhancements. "Good," he said. "We can have a chat in the morning." He picked up his briefcase and left.

Stage one successful, Sean wrote in an email to Krystyna. He had a fair idea that stage two was not far away. Once the clock had ticked round to noon, he felt a sense of nervous excitement. Would she or wouldn't she? Surely she must?

Twenty minutes later, she did. Laura stood up, put on her jacket and left. Naturally, she said nothing and Sean gave

Krystyna a thumbs-up and hurried round to Laura's desk. The computer was switched off. He opened the front door and looked out. He could see Laura walking along the street. Sean, whose knee gave him intermittent aches, was not the most mobile, but neither was a woman wearing high heels that were close to five inches. He followed at a safe distance. There was only one possible destination, which was Princes Street. This did not necessarily mean that she was going for a bus. It was possible that she might simply be going shopping. Sean followed and saw what he'd hoped he'd see. She was standing at a bus stop.

He did not want to risk walking onto Princes Street, so he hung around on the corner of Castle Street and peered round as each bus came. A few went by, but he got the result he was looking for. Laura boarded a bus to Wallyford and Sean went back to the office.

Krystyna could put the next phase of the plan into operation. She found Vince's mobile number and rang it. She hoped that he would answer it and was relieved when he did.

"I am very sorry to disturb you, but I thought it was important," she said.

Vince, who was having lunch, was none too thrilled. "What is it?" he asked.

"A courier arrived with a parcel for you," she told him.

Vince brightened up. "From Belgium?" he asked.

"Yes, it is," Krystyna said. "I think they made a mistake, so it arrived later than usual." She crossed her fingers. The last thing she wanted to hear was Vince telling her that he'd get it in the morning.

"I'll pop back in," Vince said. He would have been very surprised to see the reaction that this simple statement produced.

At ten to two, Vince walked into the office. He glanced at Laura's desk and put his briefcase on his own. He went across to Krystyna and she handed him the parcel.

"What mistake where you talking about?" he asked.

"They thought it had been delivered yesterday," Krystyna said.

Vince shook his head. "Good work," he said. He looked across the room. "Where's Laura?" he asked.

"She left," Krystyna said simply.

"Left?" Vince asked. "What do you mean, left?"

Krystyna was under the impression that what she had said was self-evident and tried to think of another way to phrase it. "Gone," she said. "Got up, walked out, left."

"When was this?" Vince wanted to know. Krystyna enlisted help.

"About twenty past twelve," Sean said. "Not that she said anything, but she never does."

"What do you mean, never does?" asked Vince, who seemed to be suffering from comprehension difficulties.

"Whenever she leaves early, she never says whether she's going home, going for lunch, anything," Sean explained.

"And does she leave early every time I'm not here?" Vince asked.

Sean and Krystyna looked at each other. Someone would have to answer.

"Put simply, yes," Sean said.

Vince sighed. "Why was I not told?" he asked, addressing his question to nobody in particular.

"It's not really my business," Sean said.

"Yes, it is," shouted Vince, "you work here."

"Yes, but I can't control what other people do," Sean said. "I can't go and drag her back into the office and tie her to the chair, can I?"

Vince needed somebody to shout at, but that person wasn't here. He settled for shouting at Sean instead. "You should have told me. You can't control what other people do, but I can. I can and I will." He marched back to his desk, opened his briefcase and slammed the package into it. He closed it again and walked to the door. He turned back and appeared to be on the point of making a leaving speech. Nothing, however, emerged and he turned again and slammed the front door behind him.

"Seems fair to assume that whatever was in that parcel wasn't delicate," Sean said.

Chapter 33

The seriousness of a situation was never more evident than when Vince eschewed a round of golf. He retired to his study, accompanied only by a bottle of water, to sit in contemplative silence and assess his options. As was his wont, he looked for someone to blame and the name of Carl Engelhamer came to mind. Vince wondered if he had, perhaps, been too slavish in his adherence to the doctrine of the American?

In fairness, he thought, it wasn't all Engelhamer's fault. Laura Fotheringham had misled him. He had put his trust in her and believed in her, but she had betrayed him on both counts. Clearly, the job he had given her was beyond her capabilities. He could, conceivably, keep her on in another capacity, but maybe a clean break would be the best thing.

All of this, he reflected as he prepared to go to bed, was part of the trials of being not only a businessman, but a visionary. It was wrong, of course, to imagine that people would be able to operate at the same level as the head of the organisation and, indeed, that was not desirable. Sometimes, though, it was natural that the leader would expect his acolytes to raise their game. He went to bed, content that he had once more shown his mettle and he slept comfortably.

Conveniently, Valerie needed to be in early on Friday, as there was a stocktaking exercise that she needed to oversee. She had anticipated that she would have to catch the bus and was rather surprised, though pleasantly so, when Vince told her that he would give her a lift. In Vince's eyes, this was a useful exercise. Not only did it give him some much-needed credit points, but it also enabled him to get to the office in time to orchestrate his plan of action.

So early was he that even Krystyna had not yet arrived. She managed to suppress her shock at seeing him so early on a

Friday, imagining that he had done so in order to facilitate an escape to the golf course in the afternoon. The sun was shining and the outside world looked more appealing than the office.

Once Sean had arrived, Vince sprang his plot. He told Sean and Krystyna that he wanted them to go out this morning and take a walk around town. Travel agents, he explained, were the area of interest. He wanted them to look at the kinds of offers and prices on show at the various travel agencies dotted around the centre of the city. This would enable him to see what kind of deals the new Golf King (Travel) Ltd could provide for its customers.

Sean, who was never comfortable until he had enjoyed his first cup of Earl Grey, wanted to have his tea first, but Vince wanted the operation to start immediately. He needed an empty office in order to undertake the difficult task that faced him and he did not want his staff hanging around while he did it.

"Take your time," he said. "In fact, take all morning. Have lunch – I'll give you expenses – and come back around two."

The offer took the edge off Sean's grumpiness. He set off with Krystyna and once they were out of earshot, Krystyna felt safe in revealing what she had been thinking about.

"I have all this information," she said. "I looked at all the websites and I spoke to people."

Sean was about to say that Vince simply wanted them out of the way, but Krystyna had read his thoughts.

"I know why he does not want us there," she said, "but what do we do now."

"We go somewhere that serves Earl Grey," Sean told her, "and then we do what we like. I don't know what you want to do, but I fancy sitting in Princes Street Gardens and doing the crossword."

Krystyna liked the idea. "I will do the easy anagrams and you can do the hard ones," she said.

"You've spent too long with Vince," Sean said.

It was a thought that was shared by Laura Fotheringham later that morning. She had arrived after ten o'clock and like Krystyna, she had been surprised to see Vince at his desk. While Laura was not the most perceptive person on the planet, she couldn't help but notice the absence of her two colleagues from the office.

Vince was not intending to turn this into a saga. "This arrangement is not working," he said. He waited to see if there was a reply, but received none. "I have to say that I am very disappointed," he went on. "You have abused my trust. I trust my staff and show them respect. I expect to get the same in return."

Laura gave him a blank look. "How?" she asked.

Vince assumed that she was referring to the abuse of trust. "You're hardly ever here," he said. "You disappear the minute my back's turned. You showed no interest in learning what we do and you've produced no work at all."

"You believe those weirdos?" she asked, waving a hand in the vague direction of Sean and Krystyna's desks.

"Those weirdos happen to be my staff and your colleagues," said Vince. "They work very hard and they do a grand job. I have to say I'm not seeing any of that from you."

"I can't work in this place, not with those two," Laura said. "I work at home."

"Evidence," Vince snapped, losing patience.

Further silence followed. Vince waited for Laura to produce some form of defence. Laura waited for Vince to deliver the knockout punch. Vince felt compelled to make the move.

"We can't make this work," Vince said.

"You're sacking me, then?" Laura asked.

"If that's how you want to phrase it," Vince said airily.

Laura looked at him briefly and then stared across the room. She sat there for a few seconds and then turned to Vince. "It's not fair," she said, her voice breaking up. "Everyone bullies me, I don't want to work here."

Vince saw tears on her face and she made no attempt to hide them. What he also saw, as she turned her seat, was the tops of her stockings. Her trademark tight skirt had ridden up as she swivelled in her chair and Vince felt the uncomfortable sensation of his anger mixing with arousal.

While being far from the world's most sensitive man, Vince was not devoid of some human sympathy and he walked across to Laura, who had now covered her face with her hands. He placed a hand on her shoulder. She did not react to it and he gave her shoulder a little rub. It occurred to him she was not wearing a bra.

"Perhaps," he said in measured tones, "we can come to some sort of arrangement."

Laura half turned and lifted her head. Unfortunately for both her and her boss, Vince had moved a little too close and Laura found herself in direct contact with the large bulge in his trousers. Vince, whose sex life had been struggling with meagre rations in the past few weeks, was unable to rein in his overexcited member and had, to his alarm, just poked her in the left eye with it.

The 'arrangement' that Vince had in mind had been nothing more than the suggestion of a financial offer. Laura, unsurprisingly, had interpreted it in a wholly different way, especially in conjunction with what had just happened to her eye.

"You filthy pervert," she screamed, leaping from her seat. "You disgusting old man," she added, as though the first statement had not made her feelings completely clear.

Vince leapt backwards and attempted to blot out the onslaught. Laura raged on for a while longer before snatching up her belongings and delivering one final tirade of abuse before she slammed the door. Vince sat down and tried to regain his composure. When he was able to begin some form of mental process again, he consoled himself with a couple of thoughts. One was that there was no possibility of his former Head of Marketing turning up in the office again. The other was that he had found a way, however unorthodox, of paying her off.

Chapter 34

Krystyna, having fulfilled her crossword duties, left the gardens and walked around Princes Street for a while. She wandered into Waterstone's bookshop and was looking at the collection of classic novels when a voice startled her.

"Okay, what have you done with him?" she heard from behind her.

She turned. "Oh, Carol, you made me jump," she said.

"That's what working with Vince does for you," Carol told her. "Perfectly sane people turn into nervous wrecks."

Krystyna had begun to understand that feeling in the past few weeks. "He was reading the paper when I left," she said, answering Carol's question.

"I've been at the library," Carol explained, "so when I heard you had the morning off, I thought we could have lunch. I'm including you, of course."

"That would be nice," Krystyna said. "But officially, I am working."

"I know," Carol said with a smile. "Sean told me what was going on. So Vince's Head of Marketing wasn't quite what he was hoping for?"

"I think she was in one way," Krystyna said.

Carol understood very well. "Body fulfilled the job spec, but the brain didn't." She glanced at the bookshelf and asked, "Buying something for your course?"

Krystyna shook her head. "No, I am just looking, really. I like the course, but you do not have time to read anything else. Always, I read the course books."

Carol understood that as well. "Sean had the same problem when he did the nineteenth-century novel course," she said. "The twelve novels and the textbooks were the only books he read in a year. I don't think he minded too much, because he'd never read eight of them and he enjoyed all of them. Well, maybe not Henry James. That was hard going, but Henry James usually is."

"No Henry James on my course, but we have Virginia Woolf," Krystyna said. "I find her difficult."

"Everyone's afraid of a Woolf," Carol assured her.

Krystyna picked up a Joseph Conrad novel and read the cover.

"Very patriotic of you," Carol said.

Krystyna smiled and said, "I have read *Heart of Darkness*, in Polish. Maybe I should read it in English also. After all, he wrote it in English."

"That's just showing off," Carol laughed. "While we're here, perhaps we could buy Vince something. A colouring book, maybe."

They moved on to a vegetarian café for lunch. Sean arrived a few minutes later and Carol got the full details of the latest events at the crazy world of Golf King Ltd.

"What's he going to do next?" she wondered.

Sean shrugged. "Who knows?" he said. "No doubt he'll find another halfwit to replace this one. Assuming that he gets rid of her, of course. You never know with him. He might keep her on for all I know, give her something simple to do. Not that I'm sure she'd be up to that, either."

"Surely even he must have seen she wasn't up to it?" Carol said.

"I don't think he was analysing her intellect," Sean said. "He'd let himself be convinced that he needed to be surrounded by babes, for want of a better word. Too much time with that American loon." He jabbed at his mushroom quiche with a fork and added, "See, this is part of the problem as well."

Carol nodded. "Revolutionary socialists always eat quiche," she explained. "And they read *The Guardian*. And drink Earl Grey." She looked at Krystyna and said, "You keep dangerous company. I'd keep away from people like him. His real name is

Ernesto, you know."

After lunch, Carol returned to her studies at the library. Sean and Krystyna headed back to the office, uncertain of what they might find.

What they found was Vince lolling in his chair with his feet on the desk, reading *The Sun*. There was no sign of Laura. He seemed in no hurry to finish his leisure break, but he put down his paper with some reluctance and said, "Quick meeting, get you up to speed."

"I had a meeting with Laura this morning and she agreed with me that things were not working out," he said, in the manner of a football-club owner reading a press release. "She decided to leave of her own volition. I accepted this offer and again she agreed that it would be better for this to take immediate effect."

Sean waited a few seconds to see if the autocue had finished. Satisfied that it had, he asked, "Does this mean that we need to get someone else now?"

Vince favoured him with a mysterious smile. "We will need an extra body," he said, "but I have been considering the way forward and I think we need to adopt a different approach." He paused for a few seconds before delivering the news. He leant forward and looked at Sean and Krystyna with an intensity that slightly alarmed them. "From now on, I will take responsibility for all marketing activity. We can bring somebody else in at admin level. That will be a more better system," he announced, with considerably more enthusiasm than grammar.

If Sean and Krystyna harboured doubts about the potential efficacy of the proposed new system, they were wise enough not to air them. Vince went on to say that he intended to employ the new person on a short-term contract and that he had drafted an advertisement. He turned to Krystyna and said, "Can you get this put into a few agencies. We need to get someone as soon as possible." With that, he said that he was calling it a day.

"Well, at least we're spared Madam Marketing from now on,"

Sean said. "Maybe you'll get your old desk back now that she's gone."

Krystyna wrinkled her nose at the idea. "I think I prefer my desert island," she said.

Chapter 35

Vince was not exactly thrilled at the thought of using an agency. The option was more expensive than recruiting directly, but he wanted somebody quickly and for a limited amount of time, at least initially. The Open Championship was looming and he anticipated a surge of interest in golf. It was unimportant that this year's tournament was being held in England. He knew that four days of high-profile golf on terrestrial television had a similar effect to that of the two weeks of Wimbledon, when neglected public tennis courts were overrun by newfound enthusiasts.

One of the other positives of using an agency was that it would involve less work. He was busy enough as it was and didn't need any more distractions. It would also mean, he hoped, that he would avoid another fiasco. He trusted that the agency would have vetted potential candidates and that he'd end up with an employee with a working brain.

What he didn't realise, having charged Krystyna with the task of dealing with the agency, was that she and Sean were adding their own validation processes. Neither wanted another Laura any more than Vince did. Their own system was a little more rigorous than the one Vince would have chosen. Vince, despite the recent debacle, still envisaged the day, outlined by Carl Engelhamer, when he would rule an empire populated to a great extent by beautiful women.

Sean and Krystyna's approach was more pragmatic. It wasn't, in truth, an onerous task, as the agency had a limited supply. It was, after all, summer, and many of their temps were busy on hospitality duty and other seasonal work. Further to that, there were men on the list and it was highly unlikely that Vince would choose one of them.

When Krystyna sent the short-list to Vince, he regarded it as though it were covered in a particularly foul-smelling substance. "Is this it?" he demanded.

"It is summer," Krystyna explained. "They have not so many people to spare."

Vince returned to the list and sighed. He would have to make do with what was on offer and he instantly disregarded the two men that had slipped through to this stage. He saw some promise in one of the two women, though his view was that she represented the least worst option. The other was married and had two children. This did not fit in with the Engelhamer Projection. He told Krystyna to arrange for the younger, unmarried and childless choice to come in for an interview.

To suggest that Lucy McGoldrick was blonde was stretching a point. Her carefully tousled hair was lightish with a suggestion of red to its hue. She fitted within Vince's age parameters, however, being in her mid-twenties. Small and slender, with an intelligent face and rather retroussé nose, she was not unattractive. Vince was not so impressed with the black trouser suit that she was wearing, but he was aware that his feet were planted firmly in the beggars' camp. Choosing was not much of an option.

He did, though, find Lucy an engaging and chatty young woman. She was a Glaswegian and had studied at Napier University. After obtaining her degree, she had stayed in Edinburgh and had worked in a couple of office jobs before boredom had taken over. Her last venture had been, by her own admission, quixotic, and had involved going into partnership with an old friend of her father. They had attempted to run an antiques business, but without a great deal of success. She was looking for something to keep her going while she decided what she wanted to do next.

Vince, whose knowledge of Don Quixote bordered on the non-existent, could see that Lucy could contribute something during what remained of the domestic golf season. The fact that she had no interest whatsoever in the game did not faze him. Sean and Krystyna had none either, and he was satisfied with the work they produced. If anything, he thought, ignorance of the game had its benefits, at least for his staff. Only one expert was required and that expert was where he should be, leading the organisation. On the plus side, she was keen on football, even though her sympathies lay with Celtic. Vince could not avoid a wry smile. A Hearts fan to the core, he would now have three Catholics working for him, even if Sean was firmly ensconced on the atheist wing of the party.

Not that he was in the least concerned by this. For all his faults – which were manifold – and his innate conservatism, he was not a religious bigot. He heartily disliked and disapproved of anything that might be described as sectarianism. He'd worked alongside plenty of Hibs and Celtic fans during his Civil Service days, so he wasn't in the least perturbed about Lucy McGoldrick's predilection for Glasgow's green side.

He decided that she would do and dispensed with the idea of letting her know by post. "I'm quite happy to have you on board," he said genially. "I'm sure you will do a grand job."

"Fine by me," Lucy replied. "When would you like me to start?"

"As soon as you like," Vince said. "We had an unexpected departure and, to be honest, we need somebody quickly. I can't make any guarantees about how long you'll be with us, but I can definitely offer you two months. Depends on how we get the overseas travel up and running."

"That's okay, I'm not looking for anything long-term," Lucy told him. "Two months is great. Next Monday all right with you?"

Vince beamed at her. "Monday's just fine," he said. "Welcome to Golf King," he added, offering his hand. As Lucy shook it, he said, "I'm sure you'll find it interesting here."

He bustled her out of the meeting room and introduced her to

Sean and Krystyna. "Lucy will be starting with us next week," he said. Sean and Krystyna adopted matching expressions of pleasant surprise. There was no gain in letting Vince see that Lucy was the only one of the agency's suggestions that they had considered worthwhile.

Chapter 36

Vince, more content now that he had a full team, called a team meeting. He viewed regular team meetings as an essential part of business management, regardless of how small the team might be. There had been occasions when he had conducted official team meetings with a single member of staff, leading Sean to wonder whether had had ever held a meeting with himself.

With four people present, this was positively a crowd. Vince set out his notes, notepad and pen on the table. All meetings were chaired by Vince and all minutes were taken by Vince. It was, he felt, only right and proper that he, as manager, not only be in charge, but be seen to be in charge.

Sean and Krystyna had, of course, seen it all before and knew what to expect. For Lucy McGoldrick, it was a new experience and one that would give her some insight of what the next two months of her life might be like.

"Welcome to the meeting," Vince intoned. "I would like to welcome Lucy, in particular, to our team and I'm sure that she will be a valuable addition to the company. It goes without saying that Sean and Krystyna do a grand job here and I have every confidence that I will be able to say the same about Lucy very soon." Lucy gave an embarrassed half-smile as everyone looked at her.

"Before we get on to Golf King business," Vince said, "I need to speak about the Health and Safety visit. This should probably go under any other business, but it won't take long and I want to get it out of the way. As you know, well Lucy won't, but as you know, we had a visit from the Health and Safety people. Just routine. I have received their report and the good news is that they are happy with what they found." He paused while his team took in the revelations and went on, "There were just a couple of things they noted. One was about boxes on top of cabinets. We mustn't put boxes on cabinets or cupboards. Everyone okay with that?"

All three nodded. Sean and Krystyna knew that the only person who ever put a box on top of a cabinet was Vince, but they were wise enough to say nothing.

"Good," said Vince. "Moving on to the second item, I was, er, it wasn't quite...er, what they say here is that we should ensure that egress is not blocked." He looked up with a puzzled expression. "What are they talking about? What's egress?"

"A female egret," said Sean, unable to stop himself in time.

Lucy tried not to laugh, but failed. Vince was left with a decision to make. Should he glare at Sean or Lucy? He decided to glare at the former, while giving Lucy a sharp glance in the process.

"Ways out, exits, that sort of thing," Sean said hurriedly.

"Why didn't they say exits then?" Vince demanded of no one in particular. "So what they mean is that they want all doors kept clear in case there's a fire or emergency. Why can't they just put that in English?"

Health and Safety information dispensed, Vince went through the agenda he had set out. Sean and Krystyna were obliged to give details of the work that they had done since the last meeting, the work they were doing currently and the work that they were doing in the future. Lucy was, naturally enough, exempt from this chore at present, but this gave her the chance to see what was required at future team meetings.

Having gleaned these details from his staff, Vince proceeded to list what had been on his plate. His plate was, inevitably, very large and it took him some time to detail his achievements. He regarded this as important; a lot of managers never bothered to tell their staff what they were up to, but that wasn't the way to run a team and gain respect. It was crucial, he felt, to keep staff appraised of what he was doing.

In terms of his future plans, he had another announcement to make. "As you know," he said, "The Open starts next week and I shall be attending all four days. Obviously, I will be watching some of the golf, but this is more about business. It's a great opportunity to network and meet people. I'm sure that I will make some great contacts and hopefully drum up some new business. I will be out of the office from Wednesday afternoon. I fly down on Wednesday and I fly back on Monday, so I won't be in the office until the Tuesday. That reminds me. Krystyna, can you make a note in your diary to print my boarding pass when it's available?"

Krystyna said, "Already, I have made a note. I put it in my calendar when I booked the flight for you."

Vince favoured her with a big smile. "Excellent," he said.

The meeting went on for almost three hours. When it finished, Vince went out to buy his usual lunchtime accoutrements, leaving three rather weary people in his office.

"Do these meetings always go on that long or was that especially for my benefit?" Lucy asked her new colleagues.

"Oh, I thought it was quite a short meeting," Krystyna said. Sean grinned.

Lucy didn't. "Please tell me you're joking," she said.

Krystyna shook her head. "Sorry, I am not joking," she said. "Ask Sean. Sean is the expert on meetings with Vince." Lucy looked at Sean, hope receding from her eyes.

"She's right," Sean said. "You should have seen some of the appraisal meetings we used to have. I had one that took over four hours."

Lucy felt as though she were becoming physically smaller by the moment, but Sean hadn't finished.

"Beware the 'five-minute chat', they're the most dangerous ones," he told her. "If Vince tells you he wants a five- or ten-minute meeting, make sure you make yourself a cup of tea before it starts. He is physiologically incapable of having a meeting that lasts less than an hour, however short he says it's going to be."

"Thanks for the warning," Lucy said. She straightened her back and stretched her small frame to its full length before adopting a boxer's pose and throwing a couple of right jabs at thin air. "I'll need to toughen up, then," she explained.

Sean nodded. "It's a good plan," he agreed.

Chapter 37

Early on a Saturday afternoon in July, the sun shone just as charitably on Edinburgh as it did on Kent. Vince was enjoying both the golf and hospitality offered by Sandwich, though his unfortunate recent experiences with alcohol meant that he found it necessary to shun the champagne tent in favour of something softer. A sponsor's cap kept the sun's rays from his largely hairless dome.

Lucy McGoldrick was avoiding the sun as well, though not by choice. Reclining on the sofa of the small flat she rented in Tollcross, she was drinking a mug of tea and perusing a small document. She was expecting a phone call and the call was late.

When the phone rang, half an hour later than planned, she muttered, "About time," and picked up the receiver. She was relieved to find that it was the caller she had anticipated rather than one of the scam artists that promised to fix her computer or mend the vacuum cleaner she didn't own.

The voice was gruff and the accent Glaswegian. "How are you getting on?" it asked.

Lucy, who did not have an abundance of patience, replied, "You're keeping me out of the sunshine, Jim."

"Then I'm doing you a favour," Jim told her. "Pale-skinned type like you doesn't need too much sun. You'll just peel."

"You're depriving me of vital vitamins," Lucy said.

"Eat an orange," Jim responded.

Lucy pulled a face and picked up her document. "Okay, are you ready?" she asked.

"What have you got?" Jim replied by way of a question.

"Something's not right," Lucy said. "The turnover isn't much. Sure, it might have gone up a wee bit in the last few months, but it's nothing special. Accounts show a tiny profit—"

"How tiny?" Jim interrupted.

"Two grand," Lucy said, "and he's even paid his corporation tax like a responsible citizen. I'm no tax expert, but that looks straight enough. PAYE system looks fair and square, too. Everyone pays their tax and NI."

Jim sighed. "So what's he up to, then?" he asked. "Big house in East Lothian, BMW – paid for – first-class travel. Holidays in Florida, Portugal, Spain, golf every time. He's got no property interests, no investments worth mentioning, no sole trade, no partnerships, just the limited company. He took voluntary redundancy. That gave him forty grand or so, but that went to the mortgage and a few weeks in Florida. Not much of that left over. Wife works in a department store, so she's not coining it. What's he got going?"

"Don't know, but he's at the golf this week," Lucy said. "Flew with BA, first-class. None of your budget airlines for The King. First-class train tickets, five-star hotel in Kent. All through the company, not his wallet. I know – I was sitting there when he told us about how this wasn't for his personal pleasure, but for the good of the company. And Krystyna showed me the bookings. I could give you the exact prices of all of them."

"Who's Krystyna?" Jim asked.

"Girl who does the admin for him," Lucy said. "That's another thing – three staff, if you include me. Can't see how he can afford three full-time staff."

"Who's the other one?" Jim wanted to know.

"Chap called Sean. He does the computing," Lucy told him.

"Pair of innocents?" Jim suggested.

"Definitely," Lucy agreed. "No way they're up to anything. I don't mean they're thick, far from it. In fact, I'd say they're way ahead of Kingmyle on the IQ front."

There was a brief silence while Jim considered what Lucy had been telling him. "How loyal are they?" he asked.

Lucy could not resist a little chuckle. Sensing Jim's surprise at her reaction, she explained, "Not much. They both think he's a clown."

"Aye, but he's the clown that pays their wages," Jim said.

"True," Lucy agreed, "but I've chatted to them. Sean's only there on a short contract and he's not staying much longer. I don't think he'd renew even if our Vinny offers him a new one. Krystyna's Polish, but she's doing a degree here and she's going back home when she gets the chance."

"At a college? Her language or English?" Jim asked.

"Open University," Lucy explained, "and she's doing it in English. And her English is a hell of a lot better than Vince's." She pulled another face at the thought of Vince's one-man assault on the language. "Mind you, that's not hard. His is shocking."

Jim had another think. "What about your IT man?" he asked.

"Old colleague," Lucy said. "Doesn't mean old friend, though."

"Any chance he might be useful?" Jim wondered.

"Well, he could be," Lucy said. "He really does think Vince is a prize wally. And he's definitely not stupid."

"Worth a few minutes of your sweet talk?" Jim asked.

"I can try," Lucy said. "He seems like a good guy. Cynical, though."

"You two should get on fine, then," Jim said.

Lucy looked at the receiver she was holding and stuck out her tongue at it. "Being cynical is not necessarily being wrong," she said. She paused a moment for effect and added, "You've built a career on it."

Jim knew when he was beaten. "Don't forget there's no obligation here. Keep digging if you want, but dig carefully," he said.

"I will," Lucy promised. She put the phone down and looked at the profit-and-loss account for one last time. She swallowed the tea that was left in her mug, even though the brew had gone cold. She didn't mind that. It was warm outside and that was where she was going.

Chapter 38

Irony does not lack for a sense of humour. Evidence of this was provided when Vince became the unwitting instrument of assistance in Lucy's plan to talk to Sean at some length.

Vince, freshly returned from the arduous business of watching golf and enjoying five-star luxury, informed Sean that he wanted a quick meeting. Sean wrote off the next two hours and joined Vince in the meeting room. After enthusing about the golf, weather, hotel, flights and all of the interesting new contacts he had made during the course of his trip, Vince told him that he had arranged to visit the golf club at North Berwick the following day and speak to the Club Secretary with a view to Golf King booking the course for clients. However, his plans had been sabotaged because of other urgent business. He did not disclose the nature of this business and Sean had more than enough sense not to ask.

"I'm so busy at the moment that I'm not going to get the chance to get over there, so I want you to go," Vince said. "You can get a train. The golf course isn't out of town, so you can walk there easily enough." He passed Sean a printed document and said, "You'll need this. I've put everything you need to ask and everything you need to check out." To make sure that Sean fully appreciated just how much work he put into the business, he added, "I drew that up last night."

Sean tried hard to keep his apathy at bay while he looked at the document. It was, in essence, a checklist and contained questions for the secretary, a list of the facilities provided by the club and any information that Vince deemed to be useful. There was space for Sean to add notes and comments to each question and category that Vince had included. The document ran to a dozen pages, printed on a single side of each sheet.

"Any questions?" Vince asked, notepad and pen at the ready.

Sean shook his head. In fact, there were several questions he would like to have asked and two stood out above all the others. He would have liked to have known what the point was. He would also have liked to have known why Vince insisted on wasting so much paper. He asked neither question.

Vince had one final instruction. "Take Lucy with you," he said. "It'll be good for her to get out and see what's going on. Give her a chance to see how we operate."

Lucy, who had no desire whatsoever to visit any golf club anywhere in the world, suddenly discovered an enthusiasm for the club at North Berwick. She had a list of questions almost as long as that of Vince, but they remained firmly inside her head.

Vince came in early the next day, but was gone within an hour. He gave no hint as to his whereabouts, but informed his staff that he would not be back in the office today and that he would see them in the morning. There would, he said, be a short debriefing meeting in the morning – assuming that he had time, which was never guaranteed – to follow up the findings of the North Berwick visit and to consider what follow-up action, if any, might need to be taken. His departure was the cue for an extended tea break.

"So, you are leaving me as well?" Krystyna said, sighing. "Everybody gets to go and enjoy themselves except me."

"Sorry," Lucy told her, "but we're playing golf today." She struck the pose of a golfer addressing a ball on the tee and performed a clubless swing.

"Nice action," Sean said. "Don't let Vince see you doing that, though. He'll drag you out for a round and I wouldn't even want to think about that experience. And I'm not playing, but you can if you like. I don't mind."

Lucy wrinkled her upturned nose. "Stupid game," she said.

"Have a look at this," Sean said, detaching Vince's document from the map he had just printed and putting it on the table in front of his two colleagues. "That should cheer you up no end."

Lucy and Krystyna leant forward and peered at Vince's list before looking at each other simultaneously. Sean sat back and enjoyed the expressions on their respective faces, which went through a range of emotions in which disbelief and contempt figured prominently.

Lucy handed the document back to Sean. "Shall we get it over and done with?" she asked, with all of enthusiasm of a vegan about to visit an abattoir.

Sean nodded and finished his tea. "Don't look so gloomy," he said. "Day return to North Berwick, standard class, no expenses paid. What more could you want from life?"

Lucy got up with a pained smile and stood behind Krystyna, before putting her hands on the shoulders of the Polish girl and bending over to whisper in her ear. "And we won't be coming back to the office, either," she said. "But don't tell anyone."

Krystyna smiled. "You will be safe," she said. "I keep secrets very well."

Lucy squeezed Krystyna's shoulders and said, "You're a pal." She collected her jacket and bag, then set off towards the station, leaving Krystyna in sole possession of the office. It was a situation with which she felt very comfortable. She made herself another cup of coffee, dug in her bag and took out the book of quick crosswords she had bought herself for occasions just like this.

Chapter 39

With time on her side, Lucy was not about to rush into the subject of Vince. She was quite happy to engage in amiable conversation as she and Sean began their mission to discover the charms, or otherwise, of North Berwick. They bought tickets and found that a train was waiting when they reached the platform.

It was, in fact, Sean that brought Vince into the proceedings. The train was chugging into the station at Longniddry when Sean waved a hand in the vague direction of the town and said, "Vince lives out this way somewhere." He looked at his companion and added, "So why he couldn't just go a few miles down the coast rather than sending you and me out here, I've no idea."

"Vince moves in mysterious ways," Lucy observed.

"You're not wrong," Sean agreed. He stared out of the train window and said, "Golf clubs, private members' clubs, Rotary Club, you name it club. Committees – he loves committees. Always has done. When we were in the Civil Service, if there was a committee going, he had to be on it. Preferably as chairman. You've been to our team meetings. That's how he likes it – chairman, minute taker, centre of everything."

Lucy followed Sean's gaze as the train pulled out again. "I can imagine him at the bar in a golf club," she said. She adopted a posh Morningside accent and said, "Pillar of the community."

"Pillock of the community," Sean said with some feeling.

Lucy laughed and said, "Why did you go back and work for him if you think he's such a bozo?"

Sean turned back to look at her and said, "I'd been thinking about looking for a short-term job and he phoned me up before I'd actually started looking. I figured that I could put up with him for a few months. Saved me all the hassle of applying for jobs."

"Fair enough," Lucy agreed.

"In some ways, he's not that bad," Sean went on. "He's a bit contradictory. Yes, he's a control freak, but if he knows you do a good job, he lets you get on with it. He's always had mood swings. Some days, he's Mr Chatterbox and then he'll have a day when he never says a word to you. I'm used to him by now, but it must be a bit weird for people who don't know what he's like."

Lucy nodded thoughtfully and decided against pursuing the topic any further for now. The train was nearly there and they had work to do. Not that Lucy felt as if she had any particular role to play in terms of serving Golf King Ltd, but she had her own objectives and it was nice to get out of the office for a day.

They walked from the station to the golf club and Sean opened his shoulder bag and pulled out Vince's list. "Let's have a wander round and tick some boxes," he said. "Then we can have a chat with this secretary fellow and that should be the lot."

"Then we can have some lunch," Lucy suggested.

Sean stopped and looked at her. "Are you hungry?" he asked. "We could have something now if you want."

Lucy shook her head. "No, I'm fine," she said. "I agree – let's get this done and then we're finished for the day."

The checklist was of such depth that it took them a bit longer than they had either hoped or expected. The Club Secretary was next and turned out to be a man that knew Vince personally. Sean was unsure whether this was a good or bad thing, but he promised to pass on the proffered compliments. By the time they had finished talking, it was after two o'clock.

"Would you rather just go straight back?" Sean asked Lucy as they left the club.

"I'm starving," Lucy said, which rather answered Sean's question.

They found a restaurant in the town centre and sat down. Lucy surveyed the menu and said, "I suppose there's no chance we get this on expenses?"

"Not much," Sean replied, "but you can try him when he's in one of his good moods."

They ordered some food and Lucy decided to dip a toe into the water. "Something puzzles me," she said. Sean looked at her quizzically and she went on, "Vince has a pretty extravagant lifestyle, I mean all the first-class travel, fancy hotels, flash car and all of that stuff, but the company doesn't seem to do all that much."

Sean made no reply and Lucy wondered whether her toe was on thin ice rather than in water. Then he leant forward and said quietly, "Do you know, that's funny? I've been thinking the same thing ever since I turned up for my first day. Smart offices in the New Town don't exactly come cheap, do they?"

Lucy felt a wave of relief sweep through her, but showed nothing externally. She was about to slide a little further into the pool, but Sean was already there.

"I know he got a decent pay off when he took redundancy," he said, "but that car of his is new and that would have eaten up the redundancy money on its own. And you're right, the business doesn't do that much. I looked up the accounts at Companies House and there's not that much going on."

Lucy was beginning to feel a sense of shock. "You looked at Companies House?" she said.

"Always do when I'm looking for a job," Sean said. "You want to know whether a company you're thinking of working for is likely to go down the tubes. Okay, I probably wouldn't have bothered if it hadn't been Vince's company. That was more being nosy."

Lucy smiled, but she was glad that Sean had taken up the challenge with such enthusiasm. Her problem now was that she wasn't sure where to go next. For now, she was enjoying her meal and contented herself with a casual comment. "Be interesting to know," she said.

Sean laid down his knife and fork for a moment. "I'm glad it's not just me," he said. "I thought I was being paranoid and cynical at the same time."

"Maybe you were," Lucy replied. "Doesn't mean you were wrong, though."

After lunch, they headed back to the station. As they waited for the train, Lucy asked, "You don't think we really are being paranoid about this, do you?"

Sean shook his head. "I don't think so," he said. "Best if we keep it to ourselves, though. Don't want Vince to find out that his loyal staff are a bunch of backstabbers."

"Well, I wasn't going to stand in the middle of Princes Street with a megaphone," Lucy said.

They took the train back to Edinburgh. Sean needed to catch another train to get home and began to feel slightly awkward. He sensed that Lucy felt the same way and their eye contact felt almost bashful. In the end, he could say no more than, "See you tomorrow, then."

Lucy smiled rather wanly. "See you tomorrow," she repeated.

Chapter 40

It was the day of the weekly team meeting and the staff of Golf King Ltd could see that Vince could barely wait. His arrival at the office was jaunty and he dispensed "Good mornings" with the bonhomie of a rich benefactor about to distribute gifts.

"Someone is happy," Krystyna whispered to Sean as they assembled at the meeting table.

"Yes, and it's not me," Sean muttered.

Vince took his seat, notes and notepad at the ready. "Welcome to the weekly meeting," he intoned. He sensed a lack of enthusiasm among his staff and set out to dispel it. "I have some good news," he announced. He paused to gauge the reaction. It was minimal and he raised the stakes. "No, I have some excellent news," he said.

The effect was not obvious, but he ploughed on. "I have reached an agreement with one of the golf clubs that I use in Florida," he said grandly. "We can therefore press ahead with the plans for overseas tours." He jabbed his notepad with his pen for emphasis and went on, "Of course, this is just a small step. A small step, but an important one. I intend to make more courses available."

Vince had not expected his team to break out into spontaneous applause or to start cheering, but he felt a little disappointed by the silence with which the momentous news was greeted. Gamely, he battled on. "Of course, it will be necessary for me to visit Florida soon. There are people I need to meet and arrangements I need to make."

"Obviously," said Sean quietly.

Vince looked at him. He knew that Sean had a tendency to sarcasm and wanted to see if his expression betrayed the emotion. Sean, however, had retained the face of an experienced poker player. Vince's close attention to Sean's reaction was good news for Lucy, who had allowed herself a smirk at Sean's remark.

"When will you go?" asked Krystyna, who had a dual purpose behind her question. She had been around long enough to know that Sean was indeed being sarcastic and that he had the ability to light the blue touch-paper of Vince's firework. Secondly, she knew that booking flights and accommodation would be her task and she might as well get it over and done with.

"It'll need to be in the next month or so," Vince told her. "Can you check flights for me? I'll give you the details of where I need to go. A week should do it. Maybe ten days."

Krystyna nodded and made a dutiful note on the meeting agenda that Vince had printed for everybody.

Lucy, who felt that she ought to contribute something, asked, "What about here? I mean, who's in charge while you're away?"

Vince waved his hand expansively. "I won't be gone long. You are all capable." He beamed with benevolence at his charges. "I trust all of you to do a grand job."

"Do you want me to put something on the website?" Sean asked.

Vince, pleased at Sean's apparent enthusiasm for the task, favoured him with his approval. "Yes, excellent," he said. "You and me can have a meeting about that. I'll give you the details and we can put something up. Good idea." He made a hurried note and went on, "We will need some good advertising as well. I have put together a few ideas."

Sean gave an involuntary shudder as he recalled Vince's previous foray into the world of advertising. Krystyna, who had also seen the unpleasant fruits of Vince's earlier labours, had similar feelings. They looked on nervously as Vince laid out several sheets of paper on the table.

Lucy, who had been about to suggest using an agency, had a sensible change of mind. She realised that Vince was likely to regard this as a personal affront, suggesting that he was not capable of producing something as good, if not better, than any of those rip-off agencies. She picked up one of Vince's prototype designs and began to wade through the peculiar form of mangled English that Vince made his own.

Vince, unable to conceive that anyone could find fault with his work, gave Krystyna another set of tasks. "I want you to look at publications where we can advertise," he said. "Golf magazines, general sport magazines, that sort of thing. Local papers as well. Come up with a list and let me see what you have. Oh, and get on to all of the golf clubs that we deal with. Find a printer to make up some posters and we'll get them put up on club noticeboards. Get Lucy to help you."

Krystyna scribbled away frantically and wondered what the likelihood was of getting any responses.

The remainder of the meeting followed the usual format and Vince concluded it after just under three hours. He had one final item, however. In the wake of his success, he had considered taking his team out for a drink, but had recalled the last occasion he'd tried that, when that Carol woman had turned up and threatened to spoil his evening. He considered making the offer with the strict proviso that it was to be staff only and that no guests were to be allowed under any circumstances. He changed his mind and decided that it would be easier to distribute some presents.

"One last thing. Wait here," he said, rising from his seat and returning to his desk. He came back with a carrier bag and announced, "In recognition of all your hard work." He gave his three staff a bottle of wine each. All of them had sufficient common sense to sound grateful.

Happy that he was leading his crew on to greater and better things, Vince went out for his usual lunchtime fare. Back in the office, his staff were enthusing about their unexpected bonuses. In the pursuit of knowledge, they were gathered around Sean's desk while he performed an internet search.

"There you are, found it" Sean said, pointing at his screen. Krystyna and Lucy leaned forward to see the page more closely.

"Stock clearance, £1.99 a bottle," Lucy read. "Aren't we the privileged few?"

Chapter 41

Since the day in North Berwick, there had been no further mention of Lucy's suspicions by either Lucy or Sean. Lucy was not at all certain that she had done the right thing. Not that she imagined that Sean would reveal everything to Vince; indeed, it had been clear that Sean, too, thought that something was not quite right.

If she was uncertain about what she had done already, she was even more unsure of what she should do next. She decided that being completely honest would be a good starting point and, when she got a suitable opportunity, she asked Sean if she could speak to him.

Krystyna had gone home, but Vince was still in the office and showing no signs of a departure, so Lucy sent Sean an email suggesting that they go to a pub. She was hopeful of a positive response and got one. Ten minutes later, she was bidding Vince and Sean a good evening.

She waited outside and Sean emerged a few minutes later. He looked at her as if expecting her to tell him what was on her mind. She read the thought and said, "Come on, let's find a pub."

They turned into Rose Street. Sean, deciding that if he was going to have a pint, he was going to have something to go with it, went to a tobacconist and bought two small, but chunky, Cuban cigars. They continued until they came to a pub which had chairs and tables outside. "Here?" Lucy suggested.

Sean peered through the window. "I see cask beer," he said. "This'll do."

A small group of Japanese tourists were the only people sitting outside and Lucy calculated that they were highly unlikely to be interested in anything they overheard. She put her bag on the table and said, "You get the beers, I'll guard the table."

"What do you want?" Sean asked her.

Lucy extracted a ten-pound note from her bag. "I'm paying," she said, "and I'll have a pint of Guinness...no, hang on, no I'll have whatever you're having. I must try to give up Guinness. They serve it so cold these days."

Sean nodded. "That's why I like beer you can actually taste," he said.

Lucy was surprised to see Sean carrying two pints of distinctly black beer. She assumed that it was Guinness. "Cask beer all off?" she asked.

"Cask beer all on," Sean replied. "This is stout. Orkney stout." He put the glasses down and gave her the change.

Lucy took a sip and held it in her mouth for a moment before swallowing. "Not bad," she decided. "You're right. I can taste something." She put her change in her bag and brought out a packet of menthol cigarettes. Seeing Sean's slightly quizzical look, she said, "I know. I do sometimes. If I'm having a drink. When I'm feeling stressed."

"And are you?" Sean asked.

Lucy nodded. "Both," she admitted. She lit a cigarette, inhaled, slowly exhaled and took another sip of her beer. Feeling more composed, she began her story.

"I felt uncomfortable the other day," she said. "I should have told you the full story, but I wasn't sure how you were thinking." She hesitated for a second to see if Sean would reply, but saw that he was happy for her to continue. "Obviously, you thought the same as me. I should have been a bit more upfront. It's a bit convoluted, but I'll tell you everything."

Sean took a drink and managed, after a minor struggle, to get his cigar going. He wasn't sure what he was in for, but whether he would like what he was going to hear was, for the present, not of great concern. He just needed to hear it.

"It's a bit labyrinthine," Lucy conceded. "A couple of weeks ago, I went for a drink with my uncle. He works in Edinburgh. Okay, more specifically, he works for HMRC. He's an inspector.

It was his birthday and he'd gone to the pub with a few of the people in his office and one or two of his friends. I hadn't seen him for a while and I told him I had a new job. He asked me where and I told him."

She leant across the table a little and lowered her voice. "Well, when I told him, I could see in his face that something wasn't right. He didn't say anything, I could just tell. We chatted for a bit and later, when a few people had left, he said why don't we go out for a fag. Then he told me. Of course, he shouldn't have told me, he admitted that, but he said that Golf King was, oh, I can't think of the term, it was being investigated."

"Enquiry case?" Sean suggested.

Lucy nodded briskly. "That's it, that's it exactly. God, you know the terminology."

Sean smiled. "Civil Service speak," he said. "I used to do a lot of that."

"Anyway," Lucy went on, "enquiry case, yeah. He's not supposed to tell people about what he's working on or anything, but it was a bit close to home. He said he'd have to pass the enquiry on to someone else. Conflict of interests. I'm a close relative. Fair enough, I said. Now you know me, well you know me enough to know that I'm a nosy bitch and of course, I asked him about what they were looking at. Basically, it was the stuff I was saying the other day. They're very interested in what our man Vince is up to, well, *if* they knew what he was up to."

Sean felt the need for a blast of Havana and a mouthful of stout. "I see," he said slowly.

"So it left both of us in an awkward position," Lucy continued. "I asked my uncle what if I found out anything. He said that was up to me if I wanted to report something. He didn't actually go so far as to tell me to play detective, but he didn't exactly discourage me, if you know what I mean."

Sean knew. "I'm glad you told me," he said.

"So am I," Lucy said. "I felt a bit bad, like I was hiding

something. I'm sorry for that. I'm sorry that I wasn't honest with you. I should have been."

"You didn't lie, though," Sean said.

"No," Lucy agreed, "I didn't lie. I just didn't tell you the truth and I'm sorry."

Sean looked at her and saw the pleading look in her rather large eyes. "Don't worry," he said reassuringly, "I'm not offended. It's not your fault that you ended up in a company that's under investigation."

Lucy managed a weak smile. "I know," she said, "but I should have told you when we went to North Berwick. I was confused, I wasn't sure how you'd react. I mean, you know Vince a lot better than me. I was even getting a bit paranoid, like you might think it was a set-up job. It's not, it was just a weird coincidence."

"What, I might think you were some kind of special agent?" Sean asked.

"Exactly," Lucy said. "I know, it's silly, but I didn't really know how to approach things." She sat back and said, "The question is, what next?"

Sean took a good gulp of his beer, surveyed the glass for a moment and finished it. He said, "I think the next thing is another pint."

Lucy was more than amenable to the idea and Sean went to the bar. She felt a wave of relief course through her and she lit another cigarette. Sean returned with two more pints of stout.

"What next?" Sean pondered, returning to the subject. "Seems to me like we've got a few options. One, we can leave things alone and let HMRC get on with it. Two, we can take a passing interest and if anything out of the ordinary turns up, we can pass it on. Or three – this is the big one – we can stick our noses in and see what we can find out. Without making Vince suspicious, of course."

Lucy considered the options, then smiled. "I like the way you said 'we', not 'you'," she said. "Makes me feel a bit less isolated."

Sean said, "Well, I'm involved now, aren't I?"

Lucy nodded apologetically. "I know. I'm sorry for that as well."

"Don't be," Sean told her. "Look, Lucy, I like you and I'm not sure what I would have done in your position. I'm glad you trust me, though."

"Thank you," Lucy said. "I do trust you. I think you're honest and I like working with you. And Krystyna as well, but I don't think I should drag her into it."

"Krystyna's a star," Sean agreed, "and no, I think we should leave her out of it. Not that I don't trust her. I do, but I think it's best we keep this to ourselves."

"Right," Lucy said. "So what option would you choose, or do you want me to go first?"

"It's okay," Sean said. "The safe option is number one. Neither of us is going to be working there for very long and we could just let things lie. Then again, because we're not going to be there for long, we could see what we can find out. I think you are similar to me in lots of respects. I've got an enquiring mind and so have you."

Lucy smiled. "That's a nice way of saying we're nosy sods, is it?"

"If you like," Sean said. "But there's no harm in that. I don't want to come over all public servant, but if Vince is robbing the poor old taxpayer, that's you and me and everyone else, for that matter. So why not look a bit deeper and see if we can find something out?"

Lucy looked relieved and said, "I agree. Let's drink to it." She lifted her pint glass and Sean clinked his against hers. "What have we got to lose?" she asked. "Our jobs are going anyway."

They had another drink and Sean decided to catch the train from Haymarket, as Lucy was walking towards Tollcross. They halted at the bottom of Morrison Street and Sean said, "Thanks for telling me everything, but honestly, I thought you were just being nosy like me."

"I probably was," Lucy admitted, "just I had a bit more reason than usual." She smiled and said, "And thank you for being so understanding. And supportive." To Sean's surprise, she put her hands on his shoulders and gave him a kiss on the cheek. There was, Sean knew, no impropriety in her action and there was none in his when he took her hand and gave it a gentle squeeze.

Chapter 42

Relationships in the Kingmyle household were of a much less cordial nature. Victoria, still working at the cosmetics shop, tended to avoid her father as much as she could. Vince had been more hopeful of Valerie's attitude towards him. The fateful night in Leith was receding into the past and a semblance of normality had returned.

When Vince informed his wife of his proposed trip to Florida, he did not expect much of a reaction. After all, he was a businessman and businessmen needed, on occasion, to make business trips. Valerie, however, appeared to be affronted by his intentions.

"Is there any reason both of us couldn't go?" she asked.

"It's business," Vince said simply.

"You'll be staying at a hotel, though," she pointed out.

"Yes, but I'll be meeting people. And I'll need to travel around," Vince argued. "You're not going to want to come to meetings and you'll be stuck in the hotel."

Valerie was still not impressed. "What's different?" she asked. "Whenever we go to Florida, you spend all day on the golf course."

Vince changed tack. "Anyway, I don't want Victoria left on her own," he said.

His wife frowned. "She's nineteen," she said. "She's got a job. She's not a child."

"She acts like one," Vince said with a hint of bitterness.

"I wonder who she gets that from," Valerie said.

Vince did not want an argument and said no more. Besides, he had lots to do and he retired to the spare room and switched on his computer. His flights were booked, his hotel was booked and all travel was arranged. That was all Krystyna's work and he opened a folder entitled 'Personnel' and a folder within it entitled

'Krystyna'. He type a brief comment, praising the efficient work she had done in sorting out his travel arrangements. He liked to record details like this, as they came in very useful for appraisals and assessments.

He noticed that he still had an active folder entitled 'Laura'. He moved this into an archive folder alongside the folder marked 'Anne'. He shook his head slowly. The two of them had been disappointments to him. True, he had not expected much of Anne. She had not been the brightest spark, but at least she worked reasonably hard and if you gave her clear instructions of what to do, she simply ploughed on with it.

He had needed something more, however, than Anne's rather bovine determination and he had genuinely believed that he had found it in Laura. Laura had, though, been a big let-down. He had been very impressed by her at the interview and he had put a lot of faith and trust in her, only for her to tip, in a metaphorical sense, a large bucket of unpleasant matter over his head.

Vince stared at the three staff folders that remained and concluded that he had a decent little group working for him. The Engelhamer concept had never really come to fruition, but perhaps it had been an unrealistic one in the context of the east of Scotland. Texas and Florida, perhaps, but maybe not Edinburgh. Even so, he thought, he had a couple of quite nice-looking girls in his office, though they didn't exactly match the original blueprint. They were both a bit too independently minded to fit that particular job description and Vince did not imagine for a moment that either Krystyna or Lucy would be likely to disport themselves in skimpy or revealing outfits, however beneficial that might be to the company as a whole.

He cast aside his brief moment of minor lechery and thought about the future of the company. If the overseas travel was going to take off – and Vince had every confidence that it would – then he would need to act on staffing. Only Krystyna was a full-time employee and there seemed to be no immediate danger of her leaving. Lucy had arrived through an agency and it should be simple enough to sign her up for a bit longer. He might even offer her a permanent post. She seemed quite a bright girl and he could see a potentially more important role for her. True, she had not seemed very interested in anything other than a short summer job, but Vince felt that she could be persuaded by a more senior position within the organisation.

That left Sean. Vince never knew quite what to make of Sean. The man seemed so lacking in ambition. He was intelligent, good at his job and he worked hard. Someone like Sean, Vince thought, should be looking to achieve far more in life. He considered the possibility of having a chat with him, but quickly discounted the idea. He recalled the time when he had recommended Sean for promotion and had made all of the necessary arrangements for facilitating the process, only for Sean to show no interest whatsoever.

"Not interested," Sean had told him at the time.

"Why?" asked Vince incredulously.

"Because I'm not," Sean replied and that was the end of that.

Vince closed his personnel files and sighed. There was no point in going through all that again and maybe it was for the best. He didn't want Sean getting ideas above his station and if he was happy doing what he did, then why not leave him to it? He could certainly use Sean's IT and organisational skills for a bit longer yet and decided that the best option might be to offer him another short contract.

Vince switched his computer off and looked at his desk diary. It was the diary of a busy man. He had a two-day marketing course to attend, then there was a trip (with overnight stay) to a golf hotel in the Borders and finally, the Florida trip. It was going to be a busy few weeks, but that, in his eyes, was one of the occupational hazards of the successful businessman.

Chapter 43

Sean recognised that glow. He had seen it many times before and it meant that Vince, to whom the glow belonged, was enthused. The glow had 'zeal' writ large in neon letters and Sean wondered briefly if he had spent two days at a particularly unstable nuclear power station. It was therefore with a considerable amount of trepidation that he asked, "Good course?"

"Excellent, thank you," Vince replied as he sat down and switched on his computer. He said, "We'll have a team meeting shortly and we can discuss it then."

Sean felt a few vital minerals ebb out of his system. He knew exactly what this all meant. As he had pointed out to Lucy on her very first day, *"When Vince says we can discuss something, what he means is that he sits there for about three hours and everyone else listens."*

Vince spent an hour giving his keyboard the opportunity to prove its resilience and then assembled his team for the weekly meeting. He dealt with the preliminaries in rapid time, being eager to get to the essential point.

"As you know," he told them, "I have been on a marketing course in Glasgow." The team knew. Vince continued, "It was very enlightening and I came away with a lot of new ideas." He looked around the table to ensure that his staff were paying attention. Satisfied that they were, he set off on his journey of discovery.

"We have a brand," Vince announced, "but do we have a strong and recognisable brand? Does our brand stand out enough? Are we a brand that is distinct from our competitors? Are we a brand that people know and trust? Are we a brand that people love?"

As Vince pumped up the volume with his series of rhetorical questions, Sean felt his willpower not only sinking, but threatening to fail altogether. He did not dare risk a glance at Krystyna or Lucy. He tried to concentrate his gaze on a spot just behind Vince's head, but felt his eyes beginning to water.

Vince, relentless, ploughed on, and Sean realised that he was no longer listening. He caught a few phrases, but the words kept coming towards him and veering over and around his head at the last moment. He wondered how his two colleagues were coping. Krystyna was sitting next to him, so he could not look at her without turning his head. Lucy, sitting a little to the side, was easier and he glanced at her. She appeared to have been turned to stone, as though Vince had reached into his briefcase and produced the head of Medusa.

"We want to be a brand that sets trends, a brand that people are proud to be a customer of and above all, we want people to say 'This is a brand for me'," Vince yelled, his enthusiasm reaching such heights that Sean had visions of The Blues Brothers and half expected Vince to leap from his chair and start performing cartwheels across the office.

Suddenly, there was silence. Vince, rather red in the face from his exertions, looked around again to see if there was any reaction. "So," he said, "you see how important good marketing is. We cannot have one iron in the fire. We need to have many of them and we need to grab them while they're hot."

Sean shuddered involuntarily at the thought of sizzling flesh, but chose not to point out the obvious and was relieved that Vince had chosen that moment to address Lucy.

"Lucy, I'd like to talk to you this afternoon," he said.

"Uh?" said Lucy, who hadn't quite morphed back into her human form yet.

"We need to have a chat about marketing. I want you to take some of this work on," Vince told her.

"Oh...right...good," Lucy said.

The team were then invited to give their weekly round-up of what they were working on and what they would be doing in the coming week. Vince went on to explain just what he would be doing in Florida and added that he was visiting a hotel in the Borders next week to look at the facilities and assess the venue. He would, he added, be talking to the Golf Manager as well. After the conclusion of Any Other Business – which Vince always seemed to have – the team retired for a well-deserved lunch break.

As soon as lunches were finished, Vince took Lucy away for the meeting he had promised. He wanted, he told her, to become involved in the marketing of the company. He could not, with his busy schedule, be expected to do all of these things by himself and therefore needed her assistance. He would also welcome any ideas that she might have.

"Depends on what sort of things we want to market," she said cautiously.

"Clean sheet of paper," Vince said, waving an A4 sheet to illustrate the point. "I think of it as an attack on many fronts. Obviously, we push the golf aspect. That goes without saying. We draw people in with the quality of the courses, the quality of the hotels and the quality of the overall lifestyle experience. We need to be seen as a brand that offers quality."

"Right," Lucy agreed, wondering how many times Vince would fit the word 'brand' into the conversation.

"There's also merchandising," Vince said. "We have experimented a little on that front already. Golf King golf balls, we provide them to customers as part of the package. Little things like that can make a good impression. People get something a little extra. They like that. I'd like to do golf tees as well, perhaps pens. Then there's clothing. We had a great success with our King of Swing polo shirts."

"Oh, I heard about that," Lucy said, perhaps a little rashly.

Vince looked sharply at her, but decided to give her the benefit of the doubt.

"There's no need to stop at shirts," Vince declared. "We can continue with shirts, but we could introduce other stuff. Umbrellas, I would like to see. Knitwear, too. Sweaters with the Golf King logo. Discreet and tasteful, of course. Wet-weather jackets, as well, maybe."

"A brochure?" Lucy suggested.

"Excellent," Vince said, noting it on his pad. "Sean can put something on the website as well. We could have a separate section for clothing and merchandise."

"Quality, but affordable," Vince said. "That has to be the aim. We don't want anything tacky associated with the brand."

Lucy was taking everything in when Vince hit her with his latest suggestion. "I thought that you and Krystyna could do a job for us here," he said.

"In what way?" Lucy asked suspiciously.

"Modelling," Vince told her. "You're both attractive young women. We could arrange for a photographer to have you modelling the clothes, holding umbrellas, that sort of thing. We could get it done in a morning."

"You want me to be a model?" Lucy squeaked.

"Why not?" Vince asked. "Only outdoor clothing, obviously. I'm not asking you to model underwear or anything." He was unable to refrain from leering slightly.

"No," Lucy said.

"One or two shots, perfectly tasteful," Vince said.

"No," Lucy repeated.

Vince frowned and sat back. "Oh, well, I can't force you," he said, "but I thought you'd like the idea."

"I don't," Lucy said.

"Up to you," Vince said airily. "Perhaps Krystyna won't mind, then."

"I doubt it," Lucy told him, "but you can try if you like." She had a sudden thought and said, "There's menswear, too. Why don't you ask Sean?"

Vince knew only too well what Sean's response would be and

suspected that Lucy did, too. "I'll think of something," he said.

If Lucy thought that was the end of the meeting, she was to be disappointed. It went on late into the afternoon as Vince laid out his plans and explained to her where she fitted into them. She had spent most of the day in meetings with Vince and began to attain some understanding of what Sean must have gone through during his Civil Service appraisals.

By the time they emerged, Krystyna had gone home and Vince was not long in following. When he'd left, Lucy told Sean about her failed career as a model. Sean listened with wry amusement as she explained Vince's schemes.

"She'll tell him exactly what you told him," Sean predicted of Krystyna's response.

"I know," Lucy said gloomily. She said, "I feel like I've been put through a mincing machine."

"Vince has that effect," Sean told her.

Lucy suddenly brightened. "I could do with a drink," she said. "Do you fancy one?"

Sean glanced at the clock. "Yeah, don't see why not," he said. He closed a spreadsheet and switched off his computer. "As long as it's a brand I love."

Lucy smiled for the first time that day.

Chapter 44

Vince was disappointed when he received a similar response from Krystyna to his plans to the one that Lucy had given. He did not understand why these women were so reluctant to take what could be a wonderful opportunity for them. Who knew where it might lead? He tended to lay the blame for Krystyna's refusal at Lucy's door, feeling that she must have persuaded Krystyna not to get involved. This, in Vince's view, bordered on intimidation and he would need to speak to her about it.

For now, though, he had bigger fish to fry. There was a golf hotel in the Borders that he was eager to see. Golf King had started to get a few bookings from people in the north of England and somewhere in the Scottish Borders would be a very convenient location. Having decided that the best way was to find out for himself, he'd told Krystyna to book a room at the hotel. He also made it known that he would like to have a meeting with the person responsible for golf matters.

Both the course and hotel were relatively new and met with Vince's approval. He'd found the course quite tough, but that was not a problem. He had a meal at the restaurant and had found no fault. The rooms were comfortable and he felt that this hotel looked like a good option for future bookings. Now it was time to make a few notes.

He found a space away from the reception area and the bar. He sat down and took out an A4 pad. There were so many plans racing through his head that he needed to write them down and find some kind of order for them.

As he made notes, he caught sight, from the corner of his eye, of a young woman wearing a black trouser suit and white blouse. She walked across to where he was sitting. Without looking up, Vince said, "Mineral water, still, not sparkling."

The was a moment's silence before the woman said, "Mr

Kingmyle?"

"Yes," Vince said, still looking at his notes.

"You wanted to talk about booking golf parties," the woman said.

Only now did Vince look up. "Oh, I see," he said. "Take me to your leader."

The woman looked puzzled. "Pardon?" she said.

"The boss man, the head honcho, the top banana," said Vince.

"Mr Kingmyle, my name is Sally Robertson—" the woman began.

"Good for you," Vince said, cutting her short. "I'm so glad to hear it." He sighed and looked sharply at her. "Look, I'm a very busy man and I don't have the time to chit-chat with secretaries. I need to speak to the organ grinder, not the monkey."

Sally Robertson kept her composure. "Mr Kingmyle, as I was trying to tell you, my name is Sally Robertson and I am the Golf Manager at this hotel."

Vince stared at her and laughed. "You're joking," he said, derision dripping from each word.

Sally opened the wallet she was carrying and held out a card. Her name and designation were quite clear, but Vince remained resolutely unimpressed.

"Then take me to someone who's got experience," Vince demanded. "A man who knows about golf." He laid heavy emphasis on the word 'man'.

"Mr Kingmyle, I know about golf. That is why I'm the Golf Manager," said Sally.

Vince shook his head. "Ridiculous," he said. "Forget it. I'll take my business elsewhere."

"That may be the best solution," Sally said.

"Still, you won't last long," Vince sneered. "A couple of months at best. I'll come back when they employ someone who hasn't just left school."

Sally remained utterly calm. "Mr Kingmyle, I have been in

this job for more than three years and I intend to continue for some time yet, so you may have a long wait. And for your information, I left school more than ten years ago, but I will take it as a compliment that you see me as much younger. Good evening, Mr Kingmyle."

She turned and walked away, taking measured paces and betraying no sign of the rage she felt inside. As she left, Vince muttered, "Bimbo." Sally caught the word, but did not stop.

Vince returned to his notepad and wrote, 'Need new venue. No point coming back here. Silly tart for Golf Manager. Waste of time.' He sighed again. That useless woman hadn't even got him the mineral water and he had to walk all the way to the bar to get one. He went to bed in a bad mood.

In the morning, Vince brought his bag down to reception to check out. He did not intend to leave immediately and asked the receptionist if he could leave his holdall somewhere. She indicated a small area, covered by a curtain, behind the reception area.

Across the foyer, Sally Robertson had seen her adversary from last night and she tucked herself behind a pillar until Vince had left the building. She had seen him leave his bag and suddenly, an idea came into her head. She permitted herself a tight little smile.

She walked across, past the reception desk and said good morning to the receptionist, before slipping into the left-luggage room. The receptionist took no notice. Sally was employed by the hotel and people were always leaving and losing things, so it was hardly unusual. Had the receptionist asked her what she was doing, Sally would simply tell her that someone had lost an umbrella or something similar and she was looking for it.

Vince's bag was not difficult to spot. The gold 'VK' lettering was a bit of a giveaway. It was, as Sally had anticipated, locked, but there was an outside compartment that had a zip fastening. Having found what she wanted, she came back out of the room.

"Should have gone to the loo before I started trying to find missing property," she said to the receptionist as she hurried to the toilet on the other side of the foyer. That ensured, she thought, that the receptionist wouldn't find it too strange when she went back into the left-luggage area again. She darted into the ladies' toilet.

It didn't take her long to do what need to be done. As luck would have it, she was wearing a skirt today and she slipped off her shoes and removed her tights and pants. She straightened her skirt and was satisfied that it was long enough to avoid potential embarrassment before she replaced her underwear. She considered taking off her bra as well, but she didn't want to make her present too bulky.

As she was about to leave the toilet, she noticed the machine that dispensed condoms. She almost laughed out loud at the thought that zeroed in on her brain. She had a utility key with her and opened the case of the machine, removed a packet and replaced the cover. She extracted two condoms and pulled them about a bit before rubbing some soapy water over them. Tucking the protectors into her discarded clothing, she moved to the next phase of her mission.

Holding her underwear beneath her jacket, she slipped behind the curtain again. She unzipped Vince's bag and slid the items in. The compartment stood out a little from the bag and she was pleased to see that there was no sign of a bulge and no suggestion of there being anything inside that pocket. It was unlikely, she thought, that Vince would open that part of the bag. For one thing, he would be putting the bag straight into his car. For another, it didn't look like he used that part of the bag at all.

She had, of course, no idea of what the outcome would be – and she would have loved to have been there to see it – but the thought amused her and it was worth the price of a couple of small items of underwear.

"Any luck?" asked the receptionist, when Sally re-emerged.

"No sign," Sally said. "Somebody lost a mobile phone. What's the betting he's got it in his pocket and hasn't noticed?"

The receptionist smiled and promised that she would keep an eye out for one.

An hour later, Vince returned and paid his bill. The sight of the youthful receptionist reminded him of something he needed to do. If Krystyna and Lucy were not prepared to do even the most tasteful modelling, then he would need to find someone who would. He tore a strip from the notepad that lay on the reception desk and scribbled 'Agency – need a girl, 20-25, maybe two girls' and pushed it into his bag.

He wouldn't, he thought, be coming back to this dump in a hurry. He collected his bag and took a quick look around to see if that annoying woman was hanging about. There was no sign of her and Vince walked jauntily to his car. "Put her in her place," he muttered to himself. He drove home, resolving to find another location with more professional staff.

Chapter 45

If Vince was under the impression – and he was – that women were making his life difficult, the following day did absolutely nothing to dispel that idea. He sat eating the breakfast that Valerie had made, taking no account that she had the day off and had got up solely for the purpose of ensuring that routine was followed. Victoria made a fleeting appearance to grab a slice of toast before disappearing to the bathroom to get herself ready for work.

"My bag needs unpacking," Vince said to his wife.

"When I get round to it," she replied.

Vince offered no further comment, but could see no reason why it could not be done immediately. In fact, he could see no reason for it not being done the night before, but let it pass. Once he had finished his breakfast, he chivalrously offered to take Valerie into town if she wanted to go shopping. She did not, though she decided against mentioning that her sole intention was to go back to bed for an hour.

He arrived at the office determined to speak to Krystyna and Lucy. He had been disappointed in the pair of them. They had been offered an opportunity presented to few and had turned it down. He found both of them in unrepentant mood. Firstly, Lucy insisted that she had played no part in Krystyna's refusal to start a life in modelling. Further to that, she observed that Krystyna was old enough and intelligent enough to make her own decisions.

Having found the feisty Glaswegian too hot to handle, Vince turned his attentions to her colleague, but had no greater success. He imagined that Krystyna, a more laid-back character than Lucy, would be more amenable to his reason, but she, too, pointed out that she was quite capable of making choices without any assistance from outside.

Vince felt rejected and could not even console himself with the thought that he would get any sympathy from Sean. It was not, he felt, worth the effort of looking there. Sean had all sorts of strange ideas. For one thing, he was a vegetarian and then there was all the arty stuff that Vince could neither stand nor understand. He was also disapproving of women being presented as sex objects and that was something else that Vince could not fathom. For his own part, he saw nothing wrong with admiring the forms of the young women displayed on the third page of his newspaper. As usual, he put all of these quirks down to the malign influence of Carol Whelan. Without her, Vince reasoned, Sean would be a different person and one that he could relate to a great deal more than he did now.

So it was that Vince spent most of the day avoiding the need to speak to anybody. He found it hard to avoid the conclusion that his staff were, somehow, involved in a conspiracy against him, albeit a minor one. In recognition of this, he decided to take a lengthy lunch at his golf club, where he sought the company of the kind of men with whom his views chimed more resonantly.

Returning to the office close to three o'clock, he had to shelve his original plan of leaving early, finding himself firstly bombarded by emails that needing to be addressed and secondly by a telephone call that went on for somewhat longer than he had hoped or expected. By the time he had finished, his staff had left for the day and he found himself in the unusual position of having to lock up.

It was a weary Vince that drove home that evening, but at least the worst was over. Such was his thought as he opened the front door of his house, but his trying day was not over yet. Not by a long way.

He found his wife and daughter sitting in the living room. Had the room possessed a thermometer, the mercury level would have been some distance below zero. Victoria left without a word and departed for her bedroom. Vince looked at Valerie and, with an air of forced cheeriness, asked, "Where's dinner?"

"Never mind dinner," she replied, "I want some explanations."

From beside the sofa, she pulled out the travel bag that Vince had used on his Borders trip. She stood up and walked to the dining table and laid down the bag.

"This," she said, dropping a pair of tights onto the table. Before Vince could even begin to think of a response, she added, "And this." A pair of women's briefs followed the hosiery.

Vince's eyes, which had something of a frog-like quality at the best of times, bulged even more prominently than usual. He took on the appearance of a curious, hybrid amphibious creature, frog eyes combining with the mouth gape of a stranded fish.

It got worse. "Not to mention these...things," Valerie said with considerable distaste as she carefully extracted two stretched and sticky condoms with a pen and deposited them on the table beside the underwear. To her amazement, not to mention chagrin, Vince laughed.

"You're having a laugh," he said. "This is a practical joke, right?" He stopped. The expression on his wife's face was the perfect deterrent. She was, quite clearly, not in joking mode.

"Well," she demanded, "I'm waiting."

"Christ, I don't know," Vince spluttered. "How, I mean who...what? ... I've no idea." He stared at the pile of evidence and wished it would go away.

"Well, they didn't get there by themselves, did they?" Valerie said.

"Obviously, someone put them there," Vince said.

"Brilliant," Valerie replied sarcastically. "Someone being?"

"Someone that wasn't me," Vince replied. Some kind of rational thought was beginning to return and he added, "Why would I put something like that in my own bag? And if I did, why would I leave it so that my wife could find it? Do you think I'm stupid?"

Valerie's look did, indeed, suggest something of that nature. She could, though, see that Vince had a point. She decided to play her joker. "And what about this?" she asked, holding up a piece of paper. Vince recognised it. It was the note he had made to remind himself to phone a model agency.

"I wanted a model," he said, with unwise ambiguity.

"This one," Valerie asked, poking at the underwear with her pen, "or was that a different one? One girl not enough for you? Quite the stud, aren't we?"

"Not that kind of model," Vince said, feeling that reason was making its way from the premises at a quicker rate than he would have liked. "A model in golf clothing."

Valerie stared at him. "You wanted a model in golf clothing. Am I married to some kind of kinky pervert? What next? A Hearts shirt?"

"No, no, no," Vince shouted, "I need models to model golf clothing. Golf King golf clothing. Models have got nothing to do with...that stuff." He forced himself to point at the ghastly array of items on his dining table.

"So she wasn't a model?" Valerie asked, her sarcastic tone undiminished.

"No she wasn't," Vince said. Hurriedly realising his mistake, he added, "I don't *know* who she was."

"Oh, you didn't even bother to ask her name," Valerie said.

"She hasn't got a name," Vince yelled, "she doesn't exist." He controlled himself and added more quietly, "That's what I'm trying to tell you. I don't know where those things came from. Someone put them in my bag."

Valerie looked hard at Vince for a long time. Finally, she said, "Clear that mess up. Victoria and I are having dinner now. You can make your own arrangements."

Vince could see that there was nothing to be gained from protraction of his defence. She would, he believed, realise that he was telling the truth and that he was in no way culpable for the curious collection of erotica that he had unwittingly brought home. For now, though, it was safer to make a strategic withdrawal.

With no prospect of getting a meal in his own house, he went out and drove to a takeaway. He bought a pizza and returned home to eat it in the privacy of his spare room. When he had finished, he unfolded the sofa bed. There was no possibility whatsoever of his sleeping in his own bed tonight nor, he suspected, for a good many nights to come. He lay on the bed, silently cursing the irrationality of women. Firstly, Lucy and Krystyna, now Valerie and Victoria.

It was during his meditations that he recalled the row with whatever her name was at the hotel. Slowly, the picture came into focus. Vince pulled the duvet over his face and groaned. There was no point even trying to explain this.

Chapter 46

Vince, consigned to a cold spare room and an even colder shoulder, had more important considerations for the time being. Marriage, he reflected, had its ups and downs, but he had always emerged intact from any previous skirmishes and was confident that he would not only survive, but prevail, on this occasion.

Florida beckoned and most of his thoughts were concerned with that project. He did, though, find time to type a long letter of complaint to the manager of the hotel that had caused him so much trouble. He neglected to mention the items that had appeared in his luggage. For one thing, all of the incriminating evidence had been disposed of and there was little likelihood of extracting an admission of guilt from the person he suspected of the outrage. For another, the subject was rather embarrassing and he would leave himself open to ridicule. He decided, therefore, to restrict his objections to the rudeness of the hotel's Golf Manager.

With his house such an unappealing prospect, Vince spent longer in the office than was usual for him. His staff put it down to the fact that he would soon be departing for the United States, and this was precisely the impression he wanted to give. He was a man of substance and it would not do for those under his control to think that he had personal difficulties. That sort of thing could undermine his authority.

At the last team meeting before his departure, he handed out instructions to each member of the team, detailing what they were to do in his absence. He had typed out individual documents for all three of them and printed each of these lists. Lucy, still relatively new to Vince's methodologies, wondered why he had not simply sent them by email. Vince gave her a brief and rather stern reply and made it clear that the way he operated was not to be questioned.

He gave his team a long and full insight into the Florida trip.

He was at pains to stress that he was undertaking this arduous task purely for business reasons. There was no personal pleasure to be had from it at all. Underlining his point, he added, "We cannot underestimate the importance of the American market."

Sean made an effort to say nothing, but failed. "We can," he said quietly.

Vince looked at him sharply. "Meaning?" he demanded.

Having let his thoughts slip out, Sean was now obliged to follow up and decided that since he had started, he might as well finish. "We can underestimate it," he said, "but we can't overestimate it. The word 'cannot' indicates the impossibility of an action."

Vince stared at him. "Would you like to chair the meeting?" he asked sarcastically.

"Not at all," Sean said, "I was just making an observation."

"You were being pedantic," Vince told him.

"You might call it pedantic," Sean replied good-naturedly, "I call it being right."

There was silence. Krystyna had adopted a sphinx mask from which no secrets could be learned. Lucy's expressive face did not possess the same degree of self-control and it was a struggle for her not to laugh loudly, let alone suppress a smirk. She contained herself well enough to look at Vince. His temples were twitching slightly and his face seemed a little pink. She risked a glance at Sean. He was looking straight at Vince and his face suggested wry amusement.

The peace was eventually broken. "If I want your observations, I'll ask for them," Vince said tetchily. Having regained control over the uprising, he continued to espouse the delights of Florida's golf courses, Florida's weather and the general way of life in that state. This was, he assured his team, exactly the sort of destination that customers wanted and it was exactly the sort of destination that fitted the image of the Golf King brand.

Now that he had built up a head of steam, he continued for

the next half hour or so in a manner that suggested he had eaten a marketing guidebook for breakfast and was now regurgitating the contents. On such occasions, he entered a zone of invincibility and untouchability that rendered him impervious to anyone or anything around him. Sean had seen it many times over many years. Krystyna was used to it by now and even Lucy, a newcomer to The Vince Kingmyle Show, recognised the signs.

The only sensible approach was to sit quietly and wait for the storm to abate. Even Vince could not go on for ever, even if it sometimes felt that way. Eventually, he brought his sermon to an end and looked at his team before inviting any comments. To his surprise, there were none. Sean had a great many that he would have liked to make, but on this occasion, managed to keep them to himself. He didn't see the need to get himself sacked just yet.

Vince continued the meeting until a point at which he began to feel in need of sustenance. Since his wife refused to make breakfast for him, he was feeling somewhat hungrier than usual, having had nothing more than a bowl of cereal. He was certainly not about to start cooking in the mornings. He was too busy a man, for one thing, and besides that, wasn't that what wives were supposed to do? At least when he got to Florida, he consoled himself, breakfast would be ready and waiting for him each morning at the hotel.

He concluded the meeting and left in search of soup. Back in the office, Lucy was thinking about stronger liquids. "It's my birthday on Friday," she announced. "You two fancy coming for a drink with me?" On receiving favourable responses, she added, "I wanted to wait until Vince had gone. I don't want him turning up. He'd just be embarrassing."

"We will say nothing," Krystyna promised.

"Good," Lucy said. "I think by Friday I'll be ready for a beer."

Sean agreed. "Never underestimate the importance of beer," he said.

Chapter 47

Vince, bound for Florida on Sunday, spent as much time as he could in the office. He had tried to prove to his wife that he was a man of steadfast disposition, rather than the shameless lothario she evidently viewed him as, by pointing out to her that he had written a stern letter to the hotel where misfortune had befallen him. It was true that he did not show her the actual letter he had written, taking the view that it may have incriminated him even further. Instead, he stressed that he had argued in the strongest possible terms that they should take more care over guests' luggage and that it was thoroughly unacceptable for respectable – and indeed, respected – businessmen to find the underwear of young women in their luggage.

Valerie listened stoically to the speech, but made no reply, at least of a direct nature. The message from her facial expression merely said, 'Unimpressed.'

Vince accepted that there was nothing else he could do, at least for now. There were too many other tasks to undertake. He had already ensured that his staff had been given precise details of what their duties were in the time he was going to be away. He had packing to do and he had people in Florida with whom he needed to liaise. All this on top of the normal everyday running of Golf King gave him no time to dwell on irritating family matters.

On his final day in the office before departure, he convened a quick team meeting to ensure that everyone was certain of their responsibilities. They assured him that they were. Taking the view that a little praise now and then was conducive to a productive working environment, he told his troops that they were doing a grand job and that he had every confidence that they would continue to do so in his absence.

In the afternoon, he embarked on something of a desk and

cupboard clear-out. Vince was not a man to throw things away lightly, but his desk drawers and the cupboards behind where he sat were bulging and something needed to go. His habit of printing out every email that he sent or received – even those arriving via an automated response – meant that space was at a premium. It was, though, with some reluctance that he set about the task. In an ideal world, he would have delegated the job to Krystyna or Lucy, but some of the documents contained information of sensitivity and it would not do for such items to fall into the hands of junior members of staff.

Having shredded a considerable pile of papers, he turned his attention to some of the detritus that was making his drawers difficult to open and close. To his surprise, he discovered that he had five staplers and he reduced this collection to one. Then there were myriad compact discs that were causing a blockage and Vince had already determined to discard these. He had copies of everything at home and it was, he considered, a safer environment for this kind of thing.

The result was that he was presently attacking a pile of CDs with the kind of vigour required to shift a golf ball from deep rough. Sean, sitting at the opposite desk and partially hidden by a partition, listened to the grunting and gasping and wondered what his boss was engaged in now. Judging Vince to be in one of his more amenable moods, he stood up and asked, "Need a hand with any of that?"

Vince looked up from his labours and replied, "No, nearly finished now. Just clearing out some old stuff I don't need any more." Sean ambled away for a cup of Earl Grey.

"What is he doing?" whispered Krystyna as she sidled up behind him. Sean explained and Krystyna said, "Oh, I thought he was having a fit." She made herself some coffee and said quietly, "He does not know that we are going to the pub?"

"Not a chance," Sean assured her. Krystyna's face could have been used in a textbook for people needing to learn how to look relieved.

Sean had expected Vince to leave early it was, after all, a Friday – but it was nearly half past four when the Managing Director of Golf King Ltd took his leave, encouraging his loyal band with one more small pep talk, a five-minute meeting that lasted, for once, for precisely five minutes. Once he had gone, thoughts turned to the celebrations planned for the evening.

Lucy and Krystyna had gone to the toilet to make themselves gorgeous, as Lucy had put it. Sean had turned off his computer and was tidying up, making sure that all cupboards were locked and everything was in its right place. He glanced at the four waste bins, filled to the brim, that were beside Vince's desk. As he did so, he noticed a CD lying on the floor, partially under the desk. He walked over and saw that it was unbroken and took it in both hands. He gave it a little bend and then thought better of it. He slipped it into a plastic cover and then into a pocket of his jacket. There was, he thought, probably nothing interesting to see, but he might as well take it home and have a look.

He switched off the lights and found Lucy and Krystyna waiting outside. "Come on, we've been waiting ages for you," Lucy said, grinning broadly. "How lucky are you, getting to escort two glamorous women to the pub?"

By way of reply, Sean offered an arm to both of them and led them off into the Edinburgh evening.

Chapter 48

When Sean awoke on Saturday morning, his head felt remarkably clear, even though his mouth felt as though some small mammal had deposited something unpleasant into it. That, along with a 'danger – full' message from his bladder, propelled him from his bed. He dealt with the more urgent need first and descended to the kitchen, where a glass of pineapple juice removed much of whatever filthy substance was polluting his tongue and palate.

Having got up, he saw no point in going back to bed. He also heard an "oof" from upstairs, followed by some muttering. Carol, it transpired, had banged her foot on a stray piece of wood that had dislodged itself from the base of the bed. Sean made a mental note to do something about it and set about preparing breakfast.

"What are you doing today?" Carol asked when she appeared in the kitchen.

"I'm going to look at that," Sean said. He tapped the CD that he had left on top of the fridge for reasons that were not now clear to him.

"What is it?" Carol asked.

"A CD..." Sean replied.

"Thank you, Professor Monaghan," Carol said. "How would a dumb broad like me have any idea?"

"It's a CD," Sean continued, "that once belonged to someone called Vince Kingmyle. He was chucking all sorts of stuff out and breaking CDs into bits. He must have dropped that one, so I thought I might as well see what's on it."

Carol allowed a slightly malicious smile across her face. "Something juicy, I hope," she said.

"Probably not," Sean said, "but it's worth a look."

"What's the betting it's blank?" Carol asked.

"Don't think it is," Sean said. "I'm pretty sure he was going to break this one up, but dropped it."

"Can I watch or is it top secret?" Carol asked.

"I don't mind," Sean said, "but let's have breakfast first."

Once breakfast was out of the way, Sean switched on his laptop and then went away to make some more tea. His computer was not the newest and seemed to take forever to reach a point whereby he could actually use it. He handed Carol a mug and said, "Let's see what we've got. This could be a huge anticlimax."

The CD, as he had suspected, was not empty. Sean was not entirely shocked to see that it contained several spreadsheets. One or two had names that meant nothing, but the was one entitled 'Charity' that intrigued him. He double clicked on it icon.

"Bugger," muttered Sean. The file was protected by a password.

"Got any clever software to get round that?" asked Carol, peering at the screen.

"No, but we could probably find some if we look hard enough," Sean replied. He sat back and thought for a moment. "Let's try the obvious first."

"Which is?" Carol asked.

Sean shook his head. "You wouldn't believe how many people use the name of their husband, wife, girlfriend, boyfriend or something like that," he said. "Let's try 'Valerie'."

He got an 'invalid password' message. "Okay, how about 'Victoria'?" he suggested. The same thing happened and he sighed. "Who'd have expected Vince to avoid the obvious?" he wondered.

"What does Vince like, apart from himself?" Carol asked.

There was not a long list of options. "Golf, football...er, that's it," Sean said. He took another few seconds to consider his next move and said, "Let's go 'Hearts'."

Once more, the password was rejected. "Is there a limit?" Carol asked.

Sean shook his head. "Not on a spreadsheet like this," he said. "It's hopeless, though. I bet we're not far off, but he could have done 'Valerie63' or 'Hearts99' or something. Might need to search for some clever tool."

"How about 'Jambos'?" Carol asked with a grin.

"Why not?" Sean said. He typed and clicked 'OK'. The spreadsheet opened.

"Woo-hoo!" Carol shouted as Sean stared at the screen in amazement.

Sean patted her knee. "Genius," he said.

The file contained a list of dates, along with the names of golf clubs. Each entry also contained a reference number that meant nothing to Sean. The dates went back over two years and the most recent entry was from six weeks ago.

"Vienna," said Carol. Sean looked at her quizzically. "This means nothing to me," she explained.

Sean tried opening other files and found that a couple were free of passwords. They looked very uninteresting and he tried the successful passwords on other files. Again, two of them opened and he found himself looking at more reference numbers. One sheet cross-referenced to the original sheet. The other listed a number of charities, also with references.

"Charity registration numbers," Sean said. He went back to the first document he had opened. "These are events," he said in a puzzled voice.

"Vince putting on events for charity?" Carol asked in an equally bemused tone.

"Not that I know of," Sean told her. He looked at the dates again. "See that last date? That's six weeks ago. I was working there by then. If there's been some event, I'd have known about it."

"So what's he up to?" Carol wondered.

So did Sean. "No idea, but I think I should have a bash at these other files."

Carol retired to work on the thesis she was writing and Sean attempted to open all of the spreadsheets on the disc. He succeeded with most of them, but found himself not a great deal wiser. More reference numbers kept appearing and apart from the charity registrations, he did not recognise the format or meaning of any of them. All he could discern was that the whole thing pointed to a number of charity events at a number of different golf clubs. By lunchtime, he was certain that he had gone as far as he could.

Carol was of a similar viewpoint. "Perhaps your little detective chum might have some idea," she suggested. "Want to give her a call later?"

"Haven't got a number for her," Sean replied. "I'll have to see her on Monday."

Carol nodded. "And don't forget me if there's a reward going," she said. "Remember who came up with the password."

Chapter 49

Sean would need to wait until lunchtime to speak to Lucy about what he had discovered, but first, he needed to ask Krystyna a question. While Lucy was busy with some post – every delivery needed to be recorded on a spreadsheet – he asked it. "Has Vince ever run any special events? I mean things like charity events at golf clubs, that sort of thing."

Krystyna looked suitably surprised. "No," she said, "I am not aware of any."

Her answer was what Sean had expected to hear. She seemed a little amused and said, "I think that Vince does not like charities so much."

"That's what I thought," Sean said.

"Why do you ask?" Krystyna wondered.

Sean knew that a truthful answer was impossible, no matter how much he trusted Krystyna. He never felt comfortable with being untruthful, but there were times when it was unavoidable and this was one of those times. "I was wondering whether we could do something like that," he said. "You know, run a charity event and get some good publicity."

Krystyna shook her head firmly. "You can try," she said, "but I would not suggest it. I think that Vince would prefer bad publicity as long as he could make money out of it. He thinks that charities are bad. He told me this, before you came here. I wanted to do something for Oxfam, but he told me that if I wanted to do this, I would have to do it in my own time. Then he started to get angry about giving money to lazy people who could not be bothered to help themselves and...well, you know how he goes on."

"Quite," Sean agreed, picturing in his mind's eye a tirade by Vince on the subject.

Satisfied that he had eliminated the hugely unlikely possibility of Vince doing something charitable, Sean sent Lucy an email asking if she was free at lunchtime. He did not go into details, but mentioned that he had unearthed something 'interesting' at the weekend. Lucy, whose inquisitiveness knew few bounds, was eager to find out more, but knew she would have to wait for a couple of hours.

Sean had ordered the coffee before Lucy arrived. The café was a good one, but the service wasn't the quickest and he had calculated, correctly, that the cappuccinos would not appear before she did. She joined him at the outside table.

"What have you got?" she asked eagerly.

Sean had seen no alternative to printing the more interesting spreadsheets and gave her the 'charity' list first. He watched her reactions, which turned from puzzlement to realisation.

"Charities?" Lucy said. "Doesn't sound like a Vince thing."

"It isn't," Sean agreed and told her about the conversation he'd had with Krystyna that morning. He was about to add more, but a waiter arrived with the coffee and he held back.

Lucy lit a menthol cigarette. "Want one?" she asked.

"Why not? Probably loads of reasons, but why not?" Sean took one and borrowed her lighter. "Any idea what those reference numbers mean?" he asked.

Lucy shook her head. "That's what I was going to ask you." She looked at the page for a few moments and picked up her bag. "We can find out, though," she added, taking out her mobile phone and dialling.

The call, Sean soon surmised, was to her uncle. The answer came within a few minutes.

"VAT references," Lucy said, putting her phone away.

Sean took a mouthful of coffee as a thinking aid. "So we're talking about VAT refunds from charity events that never happened?" he concluded.

"Looks that way," Lucy agreed.

Sean took a deep breath. "Christ," he muttered, "there's loads of them. We could be looking at thousands." He looked at Lucy for inspiration. "What do we do now?"

Lucy lit another cigarette and passed Sean the packet. "He's going to turn me into a chain smoker," she said. She looked at the spreadsheet again and said, "I think I'm going to have to have a chat with my uncle tonight. Can I take these?" She waved the spreadsheets.

Sean nodded. "Help yourself," he said. "I've got the original disc and copies at home if you need them."

Lucy put the documents into her bag. "Don't worry about them just yet," she said. "I'll take these and see what he thinks. He can check those references and have a look at the VAT records." She sat back in her chair, finished her coffee and frowned. "Did he not put any protection on those files?" she asked.

"He did. He put a password on," Sean told her.

"Which you cracked?" Lucy said.

"Sort of," Sean admitted. "Actually, I didn't. Carol did."

Lucy grinned and then looked serious. "She's not likely to talk to anyone, though, is she?" she asked.

"No chance," Sean said. "Vince can't abide her and the feeling is mutual."

"Understandable," Lucy said. "Of course, we can't prove anything. Not yet, anyway. I was thinking, was it possible that Vince was thinking about doing these events and just didn't, but it doesn't seem very likely. Or maybe just making out that he'd done a load of stuff for charity to make himself look good."

"Possible," Sean conceded. "Vince suffers from what we might call WFF."

Lucy frowned. "I think I could have a guess at what the 'W' stands for," she said.

"Not in this case," Sean said. "Wish Fulfilment Fantasy. No doubt you've heard some of his babble about all the golf courses he's played, all the places he says he's been to, all this 'played at the highest level' crap."

Lucy shuddered. "Some of them," she said. "I dread to think how many you must have heard."

"Well, it could just another symptom of that," Sean said.

"I suppose we'll just have to wait and see," Lucy said, getting up slowly. "Come on, let's get back. I've got a meeting to arrange."

Chapter 50

Vince, meanwhile, had been enjoying himself immensely. The weather had been excellent and he had played golf every day. It had taken him a couple of rounds to adapt his putting to the lightning-fast greens, but once he had found his range, his form had been impressive.

He had not achieved a great deal in a business sense, but as he told himself, these were early days and there would need to be exploratory steps before any major projects could be undertaken. Even so, he had met a number of interesting people and, as ever, had come out of the meetings with a great many new ideas. It was simply a case of taking time out to think, compute and formulate all of these ideas.

The hotel was a considerable improvement on the last one he had stayed in. His spacious room had an excellent view, a large bathroom and a television that was only marginally smaller than his sizeable bed. There were no irritating women strutting around calling themselves Golf Managers and the service was unfailingly polite. True, there had been the unfortunate incident when a maid had barged into his room to discover him lying naked on the bed with a pornographic magazine in one hand and something that was not a magazine in the other, but that was a minor quibble and he decided, generously, not to complain to the management of the hotel on this occasion.

One thing, however, was irritating him. He had tried, on numerous occasions, to telephone his wife only to find that she was not responding. He had even left a message on his home answering machine, a measure he found somewhat embarrassing. This, he assumed, was her childish response to the problems of the last few weeks. It was, he felt, absurd in the extreme that she had entertained thoughts that he had partaken in some kind of fling at that dreadful hotel. He suspected that the current radio silence was simply down to the fact that he had come to Florida on his own.

He was, of course, not to know of the dramas that had been played out in his absence. Valerie, it was true, had been ignoring Vince's calls, but that was only partly down to her determination to teach him a lesson and more because of the times at which Vince had made the calls. She certainly had no intention of getting out of bed in the middle of the night to listen to yet another description of a magnificent bunker shot or par-saving putt.

Of more concern to her was finding her daughter in a state of some considerable distress one evening after both had arrived home from work. At first, Victoria had not wanted to say what it was that was upsetting her. Valerie, though, was a woman of almost infinite patience and she slowly drew out the story. It was a story that went on for some time and one that only succeeded in Valerie's resolve to avoid speaking to her husband.

Victoria, while hardly eager to spring to the defence of her father, felt the need to tell her mother everything. The shop where she worked, she explained, had recruited a new girl who had started on Monday. At first, she said, they had got on perfectly well, but things had changed when she had seen Victoria's surname.

"She just went mad," Victoria said. "She said to me, 'Oh my God, is your father called Vince?' and when I said it was, she lost it." With some gentle coaxing from her mother, she went on to say that the girl, Laura, or was it Lauren?, somebody-or-other, it was a funny name and she couldn't remember it, Fothergill or Fotheringay or something like that, had said she had worked at Golf King and she'd had to leave because of – here she hesitated – sexual harassment.

Valerie shuddered, but encouraged her daughter to go on. Victoria continued, faltering a little as the details became more and more sordid. There was the ogling, the touching, the groping and the final straw where, Laura had claimed, she was asked to perform oral sex if she wanted to keep her job. Victoria, now weeping quietly, said that the shop manager had intervened and that after a long discussion, decided that it was not possible for the two to work together. She – Victoria – had now been given her notice and she could no longer work at the shop.

Valerie didn't know what to think. She recalled Vince telling her that he had recruited a new girl some weeks ago and that things had not worked out. Vince had said that she had not been up to the job and had been forced to dismiss her. Clearly, he was not going to admit to anything approaching the accusations that had been made, but it certainly complicated matters.

Not one to jump to conclusions, Valerie comforted her sobbing daughter as her mind raced. This, she knew, may have been no more than one disgruntled young woman making up stories simply because she had lost her job. Even so, there was an uncomfortable element of realism about some of it. She was well aware that Vince was not averse to a little lechery, but it was, in general, relatively harmless and could be curtailed by a sharp word or two. She was, however, about to get a bigger shock.

"Mum, I've got a confession to make," Victoria said very quietly.

Valerie took both of her hands into her own as Victoria began to give her the full details of the bar in Leith where she had worked. She had, she said, been asked by a friend if she'd like to work as a barmaid. Thinking that it was an ordinary, everyday pub, she had agreed, and most of the time, the pub functioned in the usual way. They did, however, have nights where the entertainment veered a little towards the racy.

Valerie took a deep breath. A bad day was getting worse and she braced herself. Victoria said that she had then been asked if she would 'perform'. She swore that she had resisted the initial overtures, but that a couple of the girls had assured her that nothing ever happened to them and that the money was a lot better than for working behind the bar. She said that she had only done it a couple of times and that had been the end of it.

"I'm glad you told me," Valerie said, squeezing Victoria's hands. "At least you stopped before it got out of hand."

"But it did get out of hand," Victoria said, somewhat timidly.

Valerie closed her eyes, but even she was not prepared for the next bit.

Victoria told her, as calmly as she could manage, about the night when her father had appeared at the pub. She had revealed so much now that there was no point in holding back. That, she explained, was her her short-lived 'dancing' career had come to an end.

Valerie said nothing for more than a minute. She knew that Victoria was telling the truth and felt no anger towards her. Yes, it had been silly, but young people did silly things and as long as they did not keep repeating the silliness, well, that was just part of growing up. Middle-aged men, however, were a different matter. They should know better, but she had the distinct impression that the older Vince got, the more juvenile he became.

It was Victoria that broke the silence. "Are you going to tell Dad what I said?" she asked anxiously.

Valerie patted her hand. "I don't think I'm in any hurry to speak to your father at all," she said. "In fact, I think it might be best if neither of us are here when he comes back."

Chapter 51

Knowing that Vince was due back the following week and with her head crammed full of new information, Lucy whispered, "Need to talk," into Sean's ear while they were making tea on Friday morning. Sean swirled a teabag around in his cup and came up with an idea.

He waited until Lucy and Krystyna were together and said, "I'm going to be here until five today, so if anyone wants to go at lunchtime, I don't mind."

Krystyna, being the most fair-minded of people, felt that it would be a little unjust to whoever was left in the office.

Sean, who had foreseen this objection, said that he was going out in Edinburgh in the evening and that there was no point in his trekking all the way home and coming back again.

"Why don't we draw lots?" Lucy suggested, as though she had just thought of it.

Krystyna agreed that this was reasonable and Sean took charge. Already with a slip of paper with 'Krystyna' written on it, he took up a pen and wrote 'Lucy' on one piece of paper and 'Krystyna' on another. As he walked behind Krystyna, he performed a quick exchange and stood between the two women, holding up a slip in each hand.

"You choose," Krystyna said to Lucy.

"That one," Lucy said, tapping Sean's left wrist.

Sean opened the paper and held it so that both could see. Lucy did a good job of feigning mild disappointment. Krystyna, ever sporting, looked faintly embarrassed, but did not need too much persuasion to accept a free Friday afternoon.

Once she had left, Sean told Lucy, "You'll make a good actress one day."

"You mean I'm a bad one at the moment?" she replied.

"No, I thought that was pretty good. Just the right level, no theatrical stuff. You've got talent; detective, actress—"

"Dogsbody," Lucy interjected.

"We're all that," Sean said. "What's the detective got, then?"

Lucy said down beside Sean at his desk and glanced around, as though she feared that someone might materialise from nowhere. She spoke quietly, but urgently. "I'm not supposed to know some of this," she said.

Sean said, "Neither am I."

"No," Lucy agreed. She had a notebook and opened it. "Right, first thing is that those VAT references were real enough. They were all for reclaimed VAT. Jim – my uncle – started going on about input tax and output tax and a load of stuff I didn't understand, but the gist of it is that those VAT refunds were made."

"To Golf King?" Sean asked.

Lucy shook her head. "No, that's the thing. It was another company." She looked at her notes and said, "Here, MG Golf Events Ltd."

Sean looked puzzled. "Who are they?"

"That's what took a while," Lucy explained. "It's registered in Guernsey and didn't show up on the HMRC systems. Mind you, Jim says their systems are rubbish, so that was no surprise. MG seems to be some vehicle for raking in money from VAT refunds. And the thing is, it looks like a one-man operation."

"The man being Vince," Sean said.

"That's the strange thing," Lucy said. "His name doesn't come up anywhere. There's one director, some guy called Mike Glyn. Registered office in St Peter Port, Guernsey."

Sean frowned. "So where does that leave us?" he wondered.

"Mystified?" Lucy suggested. She sighed and closed her notebook. "I think we just leave HMRC to keep looking. We've done what we can do. When's Vince back in?"

"He was a bit vague," Sean said. "He's flying back on Tuesday, so he might come in on Wednesday or he might come in on Thursday or he might be off for the rest of the week."

"Well, I don't think there's much else we can do," Lucy decided. "Were you really going out in Edinburgh tonight or did you make that up?"

"Oh, that was true," Sean said. "Nothing special, just a few drinks. Fancy coming? You're welcome."

"I wouldn't want to be a party-pooper," Lucy said.

"No party to poop," Sean told her. "Anyway, I know another pub that's serving Orkney stout."

Lucy smiled. "Oh well, in that case, I'm easily persuaded," she said.

Sean spent some of the afternoon trying to find something about MG Golf Events Ltd on the internet, though without a great deal of success. He was equally unsuccessful in discovering any information about the mysterious Michael Glyn.

At five o'clock, he was more than ready to leave. It had been tempting to leave early, but he had already arranged to meet Carol in town and while the thought of starting a bit earlier had its appeal, the prospect of a rough Saturday morning did not. Anyway, Lucy had popped out for a while and he needed to wait for her to return and collect her things before he could lock up.

They set off in the direction of Rose Street and Sean treated himself to a sizeable Cuban cigar that would keep him going for the evening. It was a warm, if grey, afternoon and the prospect of sitting outside with some quality beer and a good cigar was a pleasant one. They arrived at the pub to find Carol sitting outside with a pint of the fabled stout.

Sean went in to buy two more pints and returned to find Carol and Lucy poring over the crossword in *The Guardian*. "Tricky one?" he asked as he put the pints on the table.

"Nearly there," Carol said. "I just can't see this anagram. It's annoying me."

Lucy took a sip of her stout and said, "I need to go to the loo. I'll have a think about it in there."

Carol smiled and said, "Always works, thinking in the loo."

Suddenly, Sean smacked his forehead with the palm of his hand. "Got it!" he exclaimed.

"You haven't even looked at it?" muttered a puzzled Carol, but Sean had already jumped from his seat.

"Lucy, Lucy," he called, as Lucy headed for the pub's entrance. She turned in some astonishment.

"What's up? Somebody died?" she asked, smiling.

Sean took her by the shoulders and said, "Anagrams."

"Oh, come on, I'm bursting," Lucy said.

"No, anagrams," Sean repeated. "Mike Glyn. What's 'Mike Glyn' an anagram of?"

Lucy stared at him for a moment and then the letters fell into place in her mind. "Oh, my God," she gasped. She grasped Sean's head and gave him a very loud and very wet kiss on the forehead. "Be right back," she said and scampered into the pub.

Carol had watched the scene with amused bewilderment. Sean told her, "Wait till she comes back and I'll explain."

Lucy came back and Sean explained.

Chapter 52

Vince stared out of the window of the taxi that was taking him to the airport at Orlando. His gaze was somewhat wistful. The day was fine, bright and clear. Soon, all too soon, the summer would be over at home and the prospect of dark, cold days was not one he relished. One day, he thought, he would relocate to Florida. Indeed, he had taken the opportunity to look at properties in the area. Some of these were surprisingly inexpensive and his imagination had been fired.

Many aspects of American life appealed to Vince, but airport security was not one of them. He had ensured that he had arrived at the airport well in advance of his flight, which was scheduled to depart just before midday. It was a relief when he finally made it into the departures hall and once there, he bought a bottle of mineral water and sat down.

In front of where he sat, there was a duty-free shop. Vince, being a non-drinker and non-smoker, generally eschewed such places. As he watched the travellers emerging from the shop with bags of goods, he thought about Sean Monaghan. In their days as civil servants, Sean had taken quite a number of short breaks. This was one of many areas where Vince could not understand his colleague. Vince did not enjoy weekend breaks, preferring to spend at least two weeks away when he was on holiday. Not only did Sean take three- or four-night breaks, he always seemed to take them in bizarre places. Vince could see no pleasure in the likes of Sofia, Vilnius or Skopje. Why would anybody willingly visit backwaters like these? It was unlikely that any of them possessed as much as a single golf course and even if they did, the courses would be terrible.

As usual, Vince attributed Sean's stranger foibles to the she-devil that called herself Carol Whelan. He was reminded, in his train of thought, that Sean always brought back things like biscuits and chocolates from his travels. Not that he, Vince, had any interest in eating any of that strange Eastern European fare. It simply could not be trusted.

His thoughts turned to the less-than-perfect situation that prevailed in his own house and he decided, contrary to his normal instincts, that a visit to the duty-free shop might not be the worst idea. Although he was confident that everything would have settled down by the time he returned home, one or two conciliatory gifts might help to smooth things along. He bought a box of chocolates for Valerie and a bottle of perfume for Victoria, stowed them away in his hand luggage and waited for the flight to be called.

It was going to be a long day, but Vince regarded himself as a highly experienced traveller and claimed never to have suffered jet-lag in his life. Jet-lag, he maintained, was merely an excuse used by people that were lazy. When he had asked Krystyna to book his flights, she had asked whether he wanted to have an overnight stay in London before the final leg of his journey back to Edinburgh. He had dismissed the idea with a certain amount of disdain. He was quite capable of coping with two flights in a day. So what if the first took the best part of ten hours and so what if the time difference meant that his day would be extended by several hours? He was an international businessman and, as such, could deal with trivialities like these.

Despite the length of the flight, he did not sleep. He watched two movies and listened to music. He also made a great many notes, drawing up a list of activities and ordering them by priority. This he would present to the next team meeting. He had not made any contact with his staff while he had been away. This, he believed, was yet another sign of good management. It showed his people that he trusted them to do their jobs properly. What kind of message did a manager send if he was constantly telephoning and emailing people?

The plane landed at Gatwick in late afternoon. By the time he had gone through the transfer process and changed terminal, he had less than two hours to wait for his Edinburgh flight. He extracted his ever-present A4 pad from his hand luggage and made a note reminding himself to give Krystyna some praise for arranging such an efficient schedule. This was something else he would do at the next meeting. Being praised in front of your colleagues, Vince believed, was good for morale. He added the note, 'praise in public, criticism in private' before putting his notepad away again.

The Edinburgh flight was a little delayed and it was this, Vince asserted, that made him nod off on the journey. By the time he collected his bags and made it into the night air, it was almost ten o'clock. He had to queue for a taxi, an annoyance that he could have done without. Eventually, his turn came and as he sat in the back of the cab, he wondered about the kind of reception he would get when he arrived home.

As it turned out, he received no reception at all. The house was in darkness and he assumed that Valerie and Victoria had already gone to bed. He needed, he conceded, to do likewise himself and decided to leave his bags in the living room and retire to the sofa bed in the spare bedroom. As he was about to head upstairs, he spotted a note on the table in the hall. It informed him that his wife and daughter were staying at the Edinburgh flat of Valerie's sister, Erica.

Vince sighed. He thought that this nonsense was behind them now, but it appeared that Valerie was determined to spin out this hissy fit for a bit longer. Although it was late, he felt that there was no harm in a single telephone call.

"She's gone to bed," Erica told him, "and she doesn't want to talk to you anyway."

"Charming," Vince said, but only after he'd put down the receiver. There was nothing he could do at present and it would have to wait until tomorrow. Even hardened international businessmen had to sleep sometimes.

Chapter 53

When he awoke, Vince was a little disorientated and it took him a few seconds to realise that he was lying in his own bed. He rose, showered, dressed and then went in search of some breakfast, only to find that food was in short supply.

He had decided that the sensible option for today was to talk to Valerie directly. Telephone calls were not good enough. This nonsense could not be allowed to continue and he would demand an explanation. A man's wife, not to mention his daughter, could not be allowed to walk out on him without a very good reason and Vince could see no justification whatsoever for this behaviour.

At least his car was still there and he drove to a café, where he took breakfast. It was past nine o'clock now and he drove into Edinburgh, parked the car and walked to the department store where Valerie worked. On failing to see her, he had little choice but to ask one of the assistants whether she was expected in. The girl replied that it was her day off as she would be working on Saturday.

Vince returned to his car and set off for the flat of his sister-in-law. It was in the New Town and was one of those residences that had the Tardis-like quality of appearing a great deal larger on the inside than externally. He did not have many dealings with Erica, but knew that she was a rather formidable woman with an opinion of men that was somewhat coloured by a messy divorce. He would need to tread carefully.

"She doesn't want to see you," Erica said.

Vince hesitated. "Could you just tell her that I'm back from America?" he asked, a shade timidly.

"I think she knows that already," Erica told him.

At that moment, Valerie walked down the stairs. She stood at the foot and regarded Vince for a moment, then said, "It's okay,

Erica. Let him in. We need to talk, so we might as well do it now."

Erica moved aside, but with a slowness of movement designed to demonstrate her reluctance. She gave her sister a look that said, 'Bad idea,' but turned her back and made her way upstairs.

"You've got five minutes," Valerie said brusquely. She glanced up the stairs and stepped into the living room. She did not relish the prospect of Erica listening to the conversation.

"For what?" Vince asked.

"For an explanation," Valerie said. "No, several explanations." Seeing that Vince was offering no response, she continued, "I don't just mean whatever went on at that hotel. I mean all the other stuff as well."

Vince gave her a puzzled look. "What other stuff? There is no other stuff. There's nothing else I can tell you about that hotel, either. I explained that. I was set up."

"So you told me," Valerie said calmly, "and I'm not sure I believe you, but we'll move past that for now. How about strip clubs? Let's start there."

"What strip clubs?" Vince asked.

Valerie gave him a rather pitying look. "Oh, I'm sorry, lap-dancing clubs, if you prefer."

Vince knew that he would have difficulty in denying this, but did himself no favours by asking, "How did you know about that?"

Valerie gave him a tight-lipped and grim smile. "So you admit it?" she said.

Vince waved his hands in exasperation. "Yes, yes, once," he said. "I went to one once. Not on purpose. That was Stuart Webster's fault. I didn't know it was some seedy dive, I just thought it was a pub."

"But you still joined in the fun," Valerie said.

"I had no choice," Vince claimed lamely. "How do you know all this?"

"I just do," Valerie said, eager to keep Victoria out of the affair. She considered Vince's response for a second and said, "I'm prepared to believe that might have been a one-off, but I'm hearing too much that I don't like, Vince. Way too much."

"I didn't choose to go there," Vince protested. "And Webster spiked my drinks," he added, rather unnecessarily.

"Never mind that," Valerie said. "One-off visits to peep shows I can just about put up with, but sexual harassment in the office? Propositioning young women? Where does that come into it?"

Vince stared at her. "What?" he finally gasped. "Where did you get that from?" His face took on the ironic smile of a professional footballer gawping in disbelief at some fool of a referee that has had the temerity to penalise him for an offence that only 50,000 people in the stadium, along with several million television viewers, have seen.

"Where did I get that from?" Valerie repeated. "Straight from your office, as a matter of fact."

"Who?" Vince demanded.

Now it was Valerie's turn to hesitate. She was not particularly bothered about the girl that Victoria had met, but she did not want to involve her daughter too deeply. "Like I said, somebody in your very office."

"I don't believe this," Vince said. "You can't believe some fantasy. Who? I have to know. I want a name."

Valerie could not, in fact, remember the name of the girl that Victoria had told her about. All she recalled was that it was a slightly unusual name that even her daughter had been unable to recall clearly. She said, truthfully, "I can't remember her name. It's a bit of an odd name, quite a long one."

"Right," Vince said, turning away. "Right, that's it. This stops now. I'm putting a stop to all these, all these stories, all these lies." He opened the front door as Valerie stared after him.

"Where are you going?" she demanded.

Vince glanced back. “I just told you,” he said. “I’m going to put a stop to all this nonsense.”

Chapter 54

Vince had parked near Erica's flat and since he was already in the New Town, decided to leave his car where it was and walk to the office. Then he changed his mind when it occurred to him that he needed to go to the bank.

By now, it was almost one o'clock and he had no idea who would be in the office, but that was immaterial. He had identified the culprit and it mattered not whether he removed them now or in half an hour's time. This proved, he reflected angrily, that nobody could be trusted.

In the office of Golf King Ltd, Sean was reading the paper and peeling a small orange when Vince appeared. Sean was about to offer a light-hearted comment to the effect that he had not expected to see Vince this week, but one glance at his boss's thunderous visage dissuaded him.

Vince put, or rather slammed, his briefcase down on his desk and surveyed the room. Lucy was out and at first, he thought that Krystyna was too, but she emerged from around a corner carrying a cup of coffee. She, too, was about to greet Vince, but her thought processes took a similar path to those of Sean.

Vince marched across and before Krystyna could speak, shouted, "You – clear your desk and get out."

Krystyna opened her mouth, but found that she was unable to speak. Finally, she managed to stammer weakly, "Why? What have I done?"

Vince began to laugh. "Very funny," he said. "You've got five minutes. Get out and don't come back." He stomped back to his desk.

Sean had no idea of where to look. Neither did he know what to say or whether, indeed, he should say anything. He knew from experience that Vince could fly off the handle, but this was something new and he had no idea what to do.

Krystyna had walked across towards Vince and was now standing behind, and slightly to the right of, Sean. "Vince, please," she said, "tell me what I have done wrong. I do not understand."

Vince ignored her for a moment and then looked hard at her. "You don't know?" he said with a sneer. "You don't know? You make up stories and tell lies about me and you don't know. That's a good one."

Krystyna stared at him. "What stories? I have never made up stories," she said.

Vince nodded exaggeratedly. "Of course not," he said. "Running off to my wife and telling her a pack of lies." He shook his head now. "I trusted you, you know, but you've shown just what you are. Now get out."

Krystyna also shook her head, though for a very different reason. "But I have never even met you wife," she said.

Vince ignored her. He had opened his briefcase and he took out two bundles of notes. He threw them in the direction of Krystyna, who made no attempt to catch them. They fell to the floor beside her as Vince ranted, "Two months' pay. This month's and next. Count yourself lucky I'm a generous man."

"I don't want your money," Krystyna said.

"Suit yourself," Vince replied. "I couldn't care less."

Sean, who had been feeling about as comfortable as a tightrope walker caught in a gale, got to his feet. He looked straight at Vince and said, "If she goes, I go."

"It's none of your business," Vince snapped.

"Yes, it is," Sean contradicted him. "She's my colleague and I believe her. She's never met your wife. I've never met your wife, come to that, and I've known you a lot longer than she has."

"Please, Sean, don't—" Krystyna began, but was cut short by another barrage from Vince.

"Oh, so you betray me as well," he said. "I thought better of you." He produced two more wads of notes and lobbed them at

Sean. "There you go," he said, "same deal."

"Fine," Sean said, opening his bag and putting the money into it.

"And don't come crawling to me for another job ever again," Vince shouted.

Sean laughed. "Me come crawling? You were the one who begged me to come and work for you," he said.

Vince glared demoniacally at him. "Just get out, the pair of you," he yelled.

Krystyna turned on her heel and crammed a few items into her bag. While Vince continued to glare at her, Sean did likewise, slipping the two fallen bundles of notes into his bag. There were no further words. Vince glared on and kept glaring until Sean and Krystyna had walked out together. He closed his briefcase with some venom and delivered a violent kick to a partition screen, which promptly collapsed in a heap at his feet.

Sean and Krystyna walked for a minute or two and then stopped. Both of them were in a state of shock and Krystyna asked, "What was that about? What is he talking about? I never met his wife, not even one time, I swear I never did."

"He's insane," Sean decided. "Paranoia's taken over." He opened his bag and said, "I saved you something from the wreckage." He handed Krystyna the two bundles of banknotes that Vince had thrown at her. She looked at them a little reluctantly, but Sean told her, "Take them. I don't know about you, but I could do with a drink."

Krystyna smiled and put the money in her bag. Quietly, she said, "Thank you."

Chapter 55

Lucy McGoldrick was in no hurry to get back to work. It was a sunny day and she had just enjoyed lunch with an old friend from Napier University. She was contemplating an early finish in the afternoon when she saw Sean and Krystyna coming in the opposite direction.

Instinctively, Lucy knew that something was not right. Why would they leave the office unmanned? Unless Vince had called and said that he would not be back until Monday, perhaps. Even so, surely they would have waited for her to return? Maybe Vince was back already, but then again, it was unlikely that he would let them go out at the same time. No, something was wrong.

Sean greeted her with an apologetic smile. "We are now your ex-colleagues," he said.

"Oh my God, what's he done?" Lucy asked. After Sean had given her the grisly details, she looked at him and Krystyna in turn. "You wait right here," she said. "Don't move a muscle." She turned and walked towards the office, her pace a great deal quicker now.

Vince had finished performing minor demolition works, but his anger had not subsided. When he heard the front door open, he looked up sharply, but when he saw that it was Lucy, he turned back to what he was doing and ignored her.

Not that he could ignore her for long. She had opened several drawers of her desk and was putting her belongings into her bag. Vince turned his furious gaze upon her and asked, "Where do you think you're going?"

Lucy's eyes were quite large and generally gave the appearance of softness. When she was angry, however, they narrowed and at present they seemed to be little more than tiny slits. She fixed them on Vince and said, "You sacked my friends."

"I sacked one," Vince said. "The other fool decided to walk

out."

"You sacked my friends without reason," Lucy said.

"Gross misconduct," Vince said. "I run this business, I make the decisions and people will do what they're told to do. If they don't, they're out."

"Fine, then I'm out as well," Lucy said with relish.

"I forbid you to leave," Vince shouted.

"Tough," Lucy replied, zipping up her bag.

"I forbid you to leave," Vince repeated, adding triumphantly, "because you're fired." He opened his briefcase once again and threw two wads of notes onto the desk in front of Lucy. "There, two months," he said. "I don't have to do that, but I do it because I'm the best manager you will ever have."

Lucy's eyes widened now and she stared at Vince, her lower jaw slowly dropping. She gazed at him as if he were a bizarre hybrid creature that had recently been introduced to a zoo. "My God, you really believe that, don't you?" she said, incredulity spread across every word. Vince, however, was not listening and had turned away. Lucy, realising that he might change his mind at any moment, stuffed the money into her bag and rushed out.

She found Sean and Krystyna rooted to the spot where she had left them. She was happy that they seemed to be in good spirits and she smiled now. "He just threw some money at me," she said.

"And us, too," Krystyna told her.

"How much was it, anyway?" Lucy asked.

"A grand in each bundle," Sean told her "I counted it while you were taking on the Creature from the Black Lagoon."

He tapped both of them on the shoulder simultaneously. "You realise the best bit?" he said. "Roughly speaking, he's given us pay for this month and one month ahead. We've already been paid for this month. It's already in the bank. And my contract was finished, anyway, but he didn't do anything about it." He looked at Lucy and said, "And don't you get paid by the agency?"

Lucy grinned and said, "I do. And next week was meant to be my last as well." She glanced at Krystyna and said, "Sorry, we seem to have done better than you out of this."

Krystyna was smiling broadly, though. "I also got one month's extra pay," she said. "Well, thanks to Sean, I did." She explained what had happened to Lucy.

"What next?" Lucy asked. "Pub?"

"Already arranged," Sean told her.

They met Carol, who had been doing some research in the library, in a pub in the Royal Mile. Carol was already in place by the time they arrived and she watched with some amusement as Sean walked in with the two young women.

"I'd never really thought of you as a gigolo," she said. "More of a geek, really."

"He's quite an ungeeky geek, though," Lucy decided.

Carol thought about it for a second or two. "Sometimes," she conceded, before going to the bar and buying drinks.

It was left to Sean to provide the bulk of the report from the dramas of lunchtime. He had been able to give Carol the brief highlights when he had made the initial phone call, but now he was able to offer something more detailed. "We sent Lucy on in injury time," he said, passing on the baton for the final moments of the action.

It did not take Carol very long to reach a similar conclusion to the one that Sean had offered less than an hour previously. "He's off his rocker," she said.

Chapter 56

"Again?" Erica said, as Vince stood on her doorstep for the second time that day.

"I need to speak to her...please, it's important," Vince wheedled.

Erica looked at him sharply and said, "Wait," in the tones of someone addressing a recalcitrant puppy. She closed the door.

A minute or so later, Valerie opened it. "Well?" she said.

Vince glanced behind as though he were being followed. "Can I come in?" he asked. "It's important."

Valerie sighed. "I hope this is good," she said, ushering him into the living room.

"I think so," Vince said importantly. "The problem is solved. I have removed the cancer."

"What are you talking about?" Valerie asked.

"The culprit has been dealt with," Vince continued. "She admitted what she had done and I fired her. Simple as that." He permitted himself a smile of mild triumph, but it faded quickly when he realised that his wife was no so enthused by the news.

"And how did you manage to sack somebody who doesn't work for you?" she wanted to know.

Vince's eyes began their outward journey. "But you said, the Polish girl..." he stammered.

"I said nothing about a Polish girl," Valerie said. "If I recall, I said a girl with a long name that I couldn't remember, but she certainly wasn't Polish. She's Scottish and you sacked her weeks ago."

Vince's Adam's apple bounced up and down several times, but no words escaped his mouth.

Valerie stood and watched, but it appeared that Vince, for once, was struck dumb. She shook her head and said, "So, you're an even bigger fool than I took you for. Well done, that's some achievement."

"But I thought you told me—" Vince began weakly, but he was cut off.

"I did not tell you anything about Polish girls," Valerie said. "And another thing – how did she manage to admit to something that she didn't do?"

Vince swallowed, making his Adam's apple perform more contortions, but his mouth was very dry now and he made a strangle gulping noise. "I, er, well, I exaggerated a little," he said.

"You lied," Valerie interpreted.

"Well, of course she wasn't going to admit it, not directly," Vince said defensively.

"You just said she did," Valerie countered. She never took her eyes off Vince, who seemed to be getting smaller by the second. "Of course the poor girl wasn't going to admit to something she never did. She probably didn't have a clue what you were raving about."

"I misunderstood—" Vince began, but Valerie was not in a mood to let up.

"Oh, yes, you certainly did," she said, "and I suggest that you apologise to her at the earliest possible opportunity. Whether she accepts it is another thing. I wouldn't blame her if she told you to go to hell. And I'd also suggest that your other staff don't get to hear about any of this, either."

"They've, er, gone," Vince muttered.

Valerie's gaze intensified. "What?" she demanded, her voice getting louder. "Please don't tell me you've sacked all of them."

"Not sacked," Vince said, "they walked out on me. I didn't make them go. I don't see what I can—"

Valerie cut him off again. "Good for them," she said. "Very sensible if you ask me."

"I'll get them back," Vince said, his face slowly brightening. "I'll talk them round."

Valerie shook her head and sighed again. She said, "Vince,

you're living in a fantasy world. I know you've always been a bit of a fantasist, but I always thought it was pretty harmless." She turned away from him and looked out of the window, then turned back. "And there's too many lies, Vince, too many. Even now, you lied to me."

"I..." Vince began, but realised that continuing with his intended sentence was futile. He backed away towards the door and said, "I'll sort it out. I'll call Krystyna and apologise. She'll come back. So will Sean, he knows me. And Lucy. Okay, maybe not Lucy, but Sean and Krystyna, I'll put things straight with them."

Valerie looked at him with a mixture of pity and contempt. "Do you really believe all of that?" she asked, with an uncanny resonance of what Lucy had said not an hour beforehand. "Do you honestly think it's as simple as that?"

Vince stood with his head slightly bowed, but contrition was not an attribute that fitted him well. "I know it won't be easy," he conceded, "but I'll talk them round. They know me, they—"

Once more, Valerie cut him off. "They know you," she said, "that's exactly the problem, isn't it?"

Chapter 57

"Vince phoned me," Krystyna said quietly as she put her drink on the table. Those three words guaranteed everybody's attention and she continued, "He asked me to come back. He said he made a bad mistake and that he was sorry."

Carol, who had organised the night out for the Golf King refugees, said, "Vince admitted he made a mistake? Doesn't sound like him at all."

Krystyna smiled and said, "No, but you see, it was not his fault. He was given bad information, he said."

"No, nothing's ever his fault," Carol said. "What did you say?"

"I told him no," Krystyna said. "I said that I could not go back. He humiliated me. He said it was a mistake, but I said no, too many mistakes and always, he blames me. If I go back, how long until the next time? One day, two days?" She took another drink and looked at Carol. "Did he not phone you, also?"

"Not me, he wouldn't dare phone me," Carol said with a grin that suggested what the outcome would have been. "He did leave some babbled message on our answering machine, though."

"What did you do?" Krystyna asked anxiously.

"Deleted it," Carol replied.

"Well, I'm offended," Lucy said. "He didn't phone me. Obviously, I'm dispensable."

Carol grinned again and said, "You really must have upset him." She looked back at Krystyna and tapped her on the wrist, pointing to a small tape on the index finger of her right hand. "What happened there?" she asked. "Was that from punching Vince in the face?"

Krystyna smiled. "No, I broke a bottle and cut my finger," she said.

"Gave yourself a bit of a Vince Kingmyle, then?" Carol said.

She waited for Krystyna's puzzled expression before delivering the knockout blow. "A rather unpleasant prick."

Krystyna giggled and surveyed her hand, which had suffered no further damage. Lucy, however, was not so fortunate. She was in the process of taking a drink and discovering that laughing and drinking at the same time could be hazardous. Liquid flowed into tubes where liquid was not meant to flow and the resultant coughing, hacking and spluttering was only quelled by some gentle thumps on the back from Sean, who was sitting beside her.

"Sorry," Carol said as Lucy recovering to a state of gasping and wheezing. "You need more alcohol. It's the only cure." She glanced at Sean and winked. "Trust me, I'm a doctor," she added.

It took a second or two for Carol's remark to register, then Lucy's face, which had paled during her choking fit, brightened. "You got it?" she asked.

Carol nodded. "As of Tuesday. I am officially a doctor."

"Oh, Carol, well done," Krystyna cried and threw her arms around the new doctor.

"Do we have to call you Doctor Whelan, then?" Lucy asked.

"No, you call me Carol," Carol said.

"She doesn't like to brag about it," Sean said, adding, "Not more than every three or more minutes, anyway." He received a well-aimed jab on the shin for his troubles and continued, "Pity that Vince didn't boot us out this week, though. I'd have loved seeing his face when I told him."

"I'd have made him call me Doctor," Carol said with a malicious grin.

The news deserved, and received, another round of drinks. Lucy asked Carol what she intended to do now that she had completed her doctorate.

"Have a rest," Carol said. "I don't know yet. I did my thesis on women artists and I've been thinking about a book. Not just yet, though. I think it's time for a short holiday. What about you two. What's next?"

Lucy offered Krystyna the floor. "I still have my degree course," she said, "but I thought, I can do this anywhere. Everything is online, you see. I will need to come here for my exam, but I think I will go back to Poland now. Maybe I can teach English. Lots of Polish people want to learn, so maybe I can teach some of them." She sat back, then jumped forward and tapped Carol on the arm. "Why don't you come and visit me? You want a holiday, so come to Poland for a few days."

"Sounds good to me," Carol said, looking across at Sean, who agreed readily. "Where do you live, anyway? I never asked."

"Wroclaw," Krystyna said. "It is quite a big place, but perhaps you are not familiar..."

"South west," Sean said.

Krystyna nodded enthusiastically, "Yes, yes, south west," she agreed. "We have an airport and you can fly from Glasgow, so it is very easy and it does not cost so much."

"Ideal," Carol said. "We don't even need a guide book. We'll have our own personal guide."

Krystyna was delighted with her idea and then realised that she was leaving somebody out. "And you, Lucy, you can come, too. If you want, of course."

Lucy smiled and said, "Well, I'm not planning on doing anything soon." She took a drink, without any ill-effects this time and said, "All this academic stuff has got me thinking. Maybe I could do a Master's. I thought about it before, but all you clever people are giving me enthusiasm." She looked at Sean and asked, "What about you?"

Sean shrugged. "Don't know, really. A bit of IT work here and there. I'm not in any rush. Anyway, I need a few weeks to recover from the last few months." He took a big gulp of beer and said, "I wonder how Vince is getting on without any staff."

"He's probably press-ganged his daughter into working for him," Carol said, though for once, her aim was a long way off target.

"Maybe he's brought back his former Head of Marketing," Lucy suggested.

The conversation went on through the evening and drinks and good humour flowed in equal measure. Carol had arranged the occasion for a Thursday with a relatively early start, thus avoiding two potential problems, that of a Friday night in Edinburgh and of catching a late train home. Late trains, she knew, could be volatile affairs and were best avoided.

So it was that Sean and Carol were sitting in front of the television with a cup of tea, watching the end of the ten o'clock news. Sean was about to switch off the set, but decided to leave it until the local Scottish news had finished. He was only half paying attention when he heard the newsreader begin, "An Edinburgh businessman was..."

He looked up at the screen and emitted a small yelp as he saw the face projected on it. "My God, look at that," he said, but got no response. Carol had fallen asleep beside him.